TRacK & FiELd

a novel

Cormac James was born in Cork in 1971. Having lived abroad for a number of years, he recently returned to live and work in Dublin. He has had short stories published in the UK and the US, and has recently completed a commission to translate a body of Polish poetry. *Track & Field* is his first novel.

cormac james

TRacK & FiELd

a novel

NEW
ISLAND

TRACK AND FIELD
First published May 2000 by
New Island Books
2 Brookside
Dundrum Road
Dublin 14
Ireland

1 3 5 4 2

ISBN 1 902602 24 2

A CIP record for this title is available from the British Library.

The Arts Council
An Chomhairle Ealaíon

New Island Books receives financial assistance from The Arts
Council (An Chomhairle Ealaíon), Dublin, Ireland.

Cover design: Artmark
Cover photograph: Jeremy Page
Author photograph: Roddy Flynn
Typesetting: New Island Books
Printed by Colour Books, Dublin

Here is a father fashioning, limb by limb,
A body for his son. What piece is this,
Formless and horrible, torn on every side?
I do not know what part of you this is, but it is part of you:
Set it here, then—not in its own but in a vacant place.

Seneca, *Phaedra*

Night

There were steps on the boards overhead and steps on the wooden stairs and along the boards of the hall. The sound of each step was two sounds, first the heel and almost instantly but not instantly the ball of the foot, the heel slightly higher in pitch and then on the stairs the steps slower and just the ball and then heel-ball heel-ball again, approaching steadily and inevitably. The door swung open and then Dan was in the kitchen too, saying loudly and curtly:

'You right?'

Jack and I and Kate were sitting at the table. The table was bare but for the plate before me, itself bare but for the knife and fork and the little heap of bones, the tail, the spine, the fins and the head. The table was in fact a door of oak planks on the base of a table. The door was too big for the base and it always seemed a little daring to lean your elbows on the edge. Jack leaned back in his chair and looked at Dan.

'We're waiting on you,' he said.

'Well I'm ready,' Dan said.

Jack lifted his chin an inch and shouted over Dan's shoulder out into the hall: 'Moses is ready!'

'Jack,' she said, 'there are people sleeping.' She was looking at the wall as though she could see through it.

Dan smiled one of his thin smiles and jerked his head. He wanted to get on the road as soon as possible. It was already almost three and it would be light soon and he wanted to get on the road before it was light. Jack got up and took his jacket from the back of the chair and put it on. Kate made a poor attempt at not looking at him while he put it on. I was looking at the oak planks, the oak planed and sanded and painted a baby blue and the wood showing again where the blue had been worn away all round the edges over the years. Where the wood showed it was very smooth.

'Listen,' Jack said to her, 'we'll see you when we get back. We'll be alright.'

Dan was gone from the kitchen. Jack and I went out after him, up the stairs, although I had not heard his feet on the stairs. As I left the kitchen I paused at the door and turned back to her.

'We'll be alright,' I said.

Our feet were loud on the stairs, the two pairs of feet mounting the stairs at two different paces, moving in and out of phase with each other. I tried to stay in phase but the pace of his feet changed and there were only twelve steps.

The coffin was in the small bedroom upstairs. Dan was not there. The room was very small, a room that four girls had lived, in two bunks, each only five feet long and half as wide, made up especially. The bunks were gone now and there was just an ordinary single bed with an iron rail at the head and at the foot about six inches above the level of the mattress and painted grey years ago and all scuffed. The box was resting on the two iron rails and sticking out over the end and only inches short of the far wall. The room was empty but for the box and the bed and stacks of books under the bed. With me and Jack the room already seemed crowded. It really was very small. It would have seemed full with just the box and the bed.

I touched the books with my boot. 'That's not all of them, is it?'

'She's the bulk of them out the shed now,' Jack said. 'These here, we were thinking about them as weight, for the truck, the back of it.'

'And put them where?'

'This was before we saw how tight a fit it was.' He patted the lid.

Because the box was resting on the iron rails there was a space of about six inches between the mattress and the box. Jack reached in under the box and brought out a screwdriver with a wooden handle painted green. The green was worn through to the wood at the heel and where it showed through the wood was very smooth and straw-coloured.

'She's going to try and sell them,' he said. 'I told her get what she can.'

'You not going to go through them?'

The screws were sticking up all around the edge of the lid. He twisted his body and leaned over a screw and fitted the screwdriver into its slot and wrenched himself and jerked back to his original position and wrenched again and jerked again.

'Already did,' he said. 'Should take a gander yourself. A few nice books out there, even still. Were some of my own, too, I'd always wondered about.'

'I might take a look when we get back,' I said. 'But the small few I can carry back with me ... You wouldn't take more?'

He paused with his chest over the screw and lifted his eyes to look at me.

'Jim, she has nothing,' he said.

He went back to work.

'I'll take a look when we get back,' I said, but I was looking under the bed, at the spines.

'They're all library books,' I said.

'I know. If she got caught trying to sell them. I'd say half the shelves in the Royal College are empty after him.'

Dan's feet came up the stairs and he came in behind me.

'Ay-ay-ay!'

Jack paused again, his chest over the screw as before, and lifted his eyes to look at Dan. He moved nothing but his eyes.

'What?'

'You'll only have to horse it off again a mile down the road,' Dan said.

Jack stood with his chest over the screw.

'Please yourself,' Dan said.

Jack dropped his eyes again and started to unscrew the screw he'd been tightening, all his actions reversed. Dan stood watching him with his hands in his pockets. When Jack was standing upright again, Dan took his hands out of his pockets.

'Right. Two at the front, one at the back I suppose. I'll take the back,' Dan said.

We twisted and pressed ourselves against the wall to get past each other and into position, Jack and I at the front and Dan at the back. It really was a very small room.

'On three,' Dan said.

'Do you mean one two three go, or one two go?' I said.

Jack smiled into his chest.

'Just lift when I say, clown.'

The room was too small. Our backs were up against the wall and the door and the handle of the door stuck out and we were in each other's way trying to get a grip and get under the weight. The iron of the bed whined. I couldn't believe the weight of it and I was watching not to catch my back on the handle of the door.

'Suffering Christ,' Dan said, 'the weight of him.'

He shuffled sideways bringing it out from over the bed and we did our best to mirror him, trying to keep it parallel with the bed so that we could get it out straight. It had to go out the door straight or it wouldn't go at all. The door was beside the head of the bed and it had to be closed to let us at the head and once we'd shuffled out we were standing with our backs right up against the door and the door opened inwards and there was no room for Dan to move back to bring the box out of the path of the door. The room was that small.

Dan was straining under the weight. You could see the weight in his face.

'Alright leave her down leave her down lads.' You could hear the weight in his voice.

We shuffled and let it down on the rails again. The iron whined as before. Jack was breathing through his nose, and it was as though a wet sponge had been rubbed across his face.

'Christ Almighty what was she feeding him?' Dan said. He considered the box and then the door and Jack and me.

'You alright?' he said to Jack.

'I'm grand,' Jack said. He lifted his right shoulder and turned his head and pressed his face into his shoulder, darkening the cloth in a way that was nothing like his face.

Dan considered the box and then the door and Jack and me again and he considered the room generally.

'Now how the fuck are we going to do this?' he said.

'Upend our end, swing open the door, and out she goes. You take the door,' I said to Jack.

Dan considered the door.

'Try anything once as the man said,' he said.

We hadn't even lifted it clear of the rails when we realised there was no way the two of us at the front would get out the door and the stairs were even tighter and there was no way one man could take all of the weight of it going down the stairs. He was always a big man and being sick had made him even bigger, not smaller, and almost all the weight is on the front man going down stairs. We let it down again. Jack was driving the air out through his nose. His nose sounded too small.

'Slide her down, it's the only way,' Dan said flatly.

Jack was driving the air in and out of his nose. Dan considered the box and then the door and Jack and me and the room generally all over again.

'Alright, I have it, I think. Jack, you better try and keep herself in the kitchen, not to let her see it or we'll never hear the end of it,' Dan said. 'Get her to make us up more tea or some fucking thing. We'll give you a shout when we're done.'

Jack went down the stairs. The wood of his soles sounded on the boards of the landing and then the steps and then far away along the hall. Our soles scraped loudly and the wood of the box was loud on the boards. The upended coffin hit the lamp and the lamp swung back and forth from the ceiling, setting our two shadows in a dance on the wallpaper and brightening the squares where pictures had hung and bringing shadows to life under the bed and washing strange versions of the bed and the rails across the wallpaper. The sound of the wood striking the glass rang out loud and clean and sharp as a bell and everything we did was too loud. The box scraped and ground and left lines on the boards and on the edge of each step as we slid it down the stairs, shuddering at each bump. We tried to do it all as quietly as we could, and for this they'd let on not to have heard. We had to upend it to get it out the bedroom door, upend it and swivel it on the landing to turn it, and again at the bottom of the stairs to turn it out the front door. There were lines and arcs tracked wherever on the wood we'd had to shove and turn and swivel it. The weight of it was unbelievable. She had already cleared out all of his things and once the books were gone the only trace of him would be these lines and arcs on the wood where we'd had to slide and swivel it and those would be worn away again in a month. We couldn't believe the weight of it.

When Jack heard the front door open he came out and left the front door open and a lamp in the hall for light and we lifted it onto the back of the truck and pushed it as far down the bed as it would go. The wood scraped and ground on bits of gravel and dirt left on the bed of the truck even though Dan said he had brushed it out.

He had put a folded tarpaulin in the back.

'What do you want that for?' I said.

'Might come in handy. You never know.'

We breathed in the cold air, bright and bitter inside, our breaths steaming and fading and steaming before our faces. Dan had put a sheet of newspaper on the windscreen against the ice but the sheet had flapped in the wind in the night and there was a thin layer of ice on the glass under it. The paper peeled off easily, leaving its letters inverted on the ice underneath. Jack went back into the kitchen and we heard him coming out into the hall again and going up the stairs. Then the bedroom window was yellow and then it was black and we heard his shoes on the stairs again. He brought out the lamp from the hall and set it on the lid for light. There were a few coils of rope in the corner of the bed and Dan climbed up and kneeled and made it fast. We stood watching him looping and threading the rope and drawing it through, indifferently and methodically, his breath steaming and fading in the light of the lamp. The lamp

13

made brass of everything. The sky was a black violet overhead and a litmus grey in the east. Kate came out with two bulky parcels wrapped in newspaper under one arm and one hand holding a pot of steaming water and a bottle of tea in the other, holding it by the neck. I took the two parcels from under her arm. She held out a bottle of tea to Jack.

'Mind that now it's hot,' she said.

Jack took a full hold of the bottle and dropped it. Steam rose up from the spilt tea.

'You're some fucking clown Jack Larkin, you know that,' he said.

Dan looked up and then turned back to his ropes. Kate stood with her hands in her arm-pits looking down at the pieces of glass and at the steam rising up from the pool of molten brass.

'I'll clean it up after ye've gone,' she said.

'We've plenty anyway,' I said. The front door was open and it was pitch black in the hall without the lamp. Dan got down off the truck and came over to us and looked back at where he had been kneeling.

'That should hold her now,' he said.

'Jack said you wanted a pot of water,' she said.

'Anyway, we can check it when we get to Naas, say, see how she's holding up,' I said.

Dan took the pot and dabbed his fingers in it and poured it sparingly over the windscreen and the sides and flung the dregs of the pot at the back window. The steam rose up from the glass. Jack looked at the sky. We looked at the sky. Jack considered the horizons round about, the east last. Kate took her hands from her armpits and took back the empty steaming pot from Dan and disappeared into the blackness of the hall. Jack looked at me and then looked at where she had stood. I could hear the last of the water dripping from the running board, its slow tick.

She appeared at the front door again, solid brass in the lamp-light and framed in the doorway with the blackness behind and she came forwards with an unlabelled jam-jar half-full with a clear liquid and the cap in the same hand and she dabbed her fingers and flicked it above our heads, her fingers flicking the way they flicked when she was wetting dough. She walked to the side of the truck and flicked her fingers. She was not looking at us or at the final destination of the water, only its initial trajectory, upwards and off into the distance. She turned and started to flick at us again.

'Jesus Christ woman, we'll have enough trouble without you drowning us first,' Dan said, and turned away.

The three of us got into the cab of the truck. Jack caught my eye and shook his head discreetly. I was in the middle. Dan was in the driver's seat.

'Can you not push in more?' Jack said.

'This is as small as I get,' I said.

Jack closed the door quietly. Dan slammed the door and rolled down the window and she came up alongside.

'We'll be grand,' Dan said. 'We'll see you Thursday so.

'Please God,' she said.

He gave her some sort of smile and started the engine and listened to it and flicked on the lights. The engine was loud in the night. The houses all about were black, the road, the sky, all black, but none of them the same. Yet it was not always clear where one left off and another began. The headlights seemed only to penetrate the night a short distance, as if in fog, and the houses at the end of the street and to the side, beyond the reach of the lights, seemed no less black than before, no less a part of the night. But the houses were there, solid and present in the darkness. Now that the bedroom window was black, there were no squares of yellow on the street. We wouldn't see a square of yellow until we turned the first corner. Dan waited until we'd turned the first corner before he began to roll up the window again.

Night—Dawn

'Leave that down, will you?' Jack said.

Dan rolled the window back down a few inches.

'Christ, are you very bad?' he said.

'The head on him,' I said. 'He's dying.'

'Just let me get settled, get used to it.'

'And I suppose you put nothing inside yourself either, this morning now?' Dan said.

'I had a bit.'

'A corner of toast he had and maybe two slugs of tea,' I said.

The night air was cold and it played with the hair that stuck out from under our caps.

'I suppose I'd be wasting my breath saying anything,' Dan said.

'You would,' Jack said.

I was watching Jack out of the corner of my eye. I didn't want him to see me watching him. He didn't want to talk. He had his eyes fixed on a cigarette burn on the dash and he needed to keep his mind on that spot, away from everything it was not.

'We started over in Clancy's house,' I said. 'With some of his own stuff.'

Dan groaned.

'Did you get any sleep at all? I never heard you come in.' Dan said. 'I heard you alright about eleven,' he said to me.

'It was more like twelve. This gentleman,' I said, 'was going to have one more and he'd follow me right home. Right home.'

'Famous last words.'

'I got a few hours,' Jack said.

'Well if you want to stop just shout,' Dan said.

'Don't worry. You'll be the first to know.'

There was no traffic. Between home and Dolphin's Barn we passed maybe three bicycles and as many carts and after that we passed nothing at all for four or five miles. The city roads and the roads leading out of the city were good compared to what we would meet in the country and once the engine was warmed up Dan didn't hold back and we were fairly racketting along. He knew this was the time to make time, as much as we could while we could.

'What was she feeding him?' Dan said, shaking his head. 'He didn't starve anyway? Give her that.'

The engine was an alien sound in the quiet that would bring on the dawn and the quietness impressed us and we didn't talk much at first. More of the vault of the sky was more grey than black now, the litmus grey soaking higher and higher, warmest in the east, throwing the buildings all around into relief so they seemed blacker than before and robbed of all detail, mere flat, black silhouettes against the grey vault of the sky.

'I'm frozen,' I said.

'Go on, I'm alright now,' Jack said.

Dan rolled up the window, shutting out a world of sound. Even the sound of the engine was changed. We sat shapeless beneath an old army blanket doubled over and laid across our knees and overcoats and scarves and caps and Jack and I with our hands in our armpits. It was much warmer and quieter with the window up.

An army truck passed us headed into the city, the back uncovered, still too dark to see who was in the back, only that they were the right shape and size.

'Ye're up very early lads,' I said.

'Or very late,' Jack said.

'The early bird,' Dan said.

'Or the very late one,' Jack said.

'Will some one of ye turn him the fuck off,' Dan said.

We watched the truck pass and listened to the sound of the truck fade behind us. I leaned back, as if I was relaxing. I wanted to see if Dan glanced in the mirror.

'Isn't McCarthy a gas fucking man all the same, isn't he?' Dan said, looking into the mirror. 'Of course he's coming. Oh he's all on for it. Wouldn't have it any other way. Nothing only all oul guff. Bad bastard.'

Jack and I said nothing.

'Well brave he was, when it was all still talk.'

'And where were you thinking of putting him, with me here?' I said. 'You're disappointed, is that what you're trying to tell me?'

'He pulled out before we even knew for sure you'd get here.'

'Well, here I am.'

Jack said nothing. He just kept his hands in his lap, turning and turning his wedding-ring.

'Well brave.'

'Alright Dan,' I said.

'What?' he said.

'I said alright. We're after going over it and over it. There's fuck all we can do now.'

'Christ Almighty. All I'm saying is McCarthy ...'

Jack and I stared at the road ahead. Dan was in the driver's seat, so he had to stare at it.

'It's the taste of it in your mouth,' Jack said. He was investigating his gums with his tongue. He elbowed me hard in the side: 'Time gents please now.'

I had looked at my watch a few minutes before. 'It's early yet,' I said.

'What time are we due?'

'I said they'd see us when they saw us,' Dan said. 'I said it might well be tomorrow, more like than not. I told them not to have anything ready or anything, we didn't know what time we'd be.'

'Neither the day nor the hour,' I said.

In the night under the moon and the stars everything had been black and you could see everything. Now there was nothing like a sun or heat or light from the sky but everything was grey, the houses and the road and the ditches and the fields and the hills beyond the houses, all different greys, each melting into the next. Only the mountains to the south-east were still black, between us and the sun.

'How are we for eats?' I said.

'You savage,' Dan said. 'And only after a feed.'

'For later I'm saying.'

'She's after making up a feast. There's gallons of tea and sandwiches and stuff for to make ourselves later. We'll stop and light a fire in the afternoon sometime,' Dan said.

After a while Jack said: 'I need a drink of water.'

We were on a dangerous curve, just down from the brow of a hill.

'We'll pull up a bit here now,' Dan said.

We went over the hill and pulled in a few hundred yards

down the road. Jack opened the door a foot and twisted and leaned out with his back to us, pulling the blanket off Dan's knees and looking back along the outside of the truck as if checking the wheels and his head dropped and shuddered and then there was the sound of his throat and the sound of it hitting the ground, like water on stone. He was silent and still and then he dropped his head and shuddered again. There was a lot of it. We left him alone and let him get on with it. After two or three more times, he dropped his head and there was the sound of his throat but no other sound. He was empty.

'The challenge of self-government now lies at the feet of every Irishman,' I said. That was a joke.

Dan rubbed his eyes with the butt of his hand and looked at the road ahead. The western horizon was still dark. Jack pushed the door open a little more and got out and walked slowly over to the ditch and stood there with his back to us, his hands on his thighs like a tired runner. Dan turned the engine off and got out and I got out Dan's door. There was a seaman's trunk bolted to the bed of the truck for tools and such and that was where we'd put all our parcels and sundries. He got a bottle out of the trunk. It was an old Tyrconnell bottle filled with water. He went over to the ditch and held the bottle out to Jack.

'Good luck,' Jack said. He tilted the bottle and his head and poured, making sure not to touch the mouth of it to his mouth. He flushed the water round his mouth and spat and looked at the label and raised his eyebrows. Waiting, we looked away from him and each other and back towards home. We heard him drink again and this time he did not spit. He gave Dan back the bottle and nodded. He leaned over again with his hands on his thighs. Dan put the flat of his hand between Jack's shoulder blades.

'You'll be better now you got that off you,' he said.

After a minute Jack stood and drank again and spat and wiped his mouth with his sleeve. I could hear him breathing hard through his nose. When his breathing was quieter we got back in the truck and went on, the brightest part of the sky behind us.

'I remember one time when I was just starting drinking,' Dan said. 'I was fourteen or fifteen I suppose, and I was out with Jack Ryan this night. You remember Ryan.'

'Turned out a great little hurler,' Jack said.

I knew I had played with him on a school team and knew who they were talking about, but I couldn't remember his face. I remembered a pair of buckled shoes he'd had for his First Communion but I couldn't remember his face.

'That's the man,' Dan said. 'Anyway, we used drink down this dive off Camden Street. And we'd been at it from early evening this night and I was well on when I got home. In bits I was. And it pissing out of the heavens. Somehow, don't ask me how, I got myself in the door and up the stairs and into the bed and out like a light. I was sleeping in the back bedroom those days, with our friend here. Only the middle of the night I came to again. Felt like I was after coming back from the dead. And you know the way you're lying there and you know. If you don't move you'll be alright for a bit, but sooner or later the bucket's coming up out of the well. I knew there was no way I'd make it to the yard.'

'This is the one about getting you sick out the window and the rain washing it away, and then me trying to do the same a week later,' Jack said. 'Sure you told us this one I don't know how many times.'

'Go on and don't mind him,' I said.

'How was I meant to know there'd be no rain?' Jack said.

'Jack,' Dan said.

'Or maybe it was my fault it didn't rain that night?'

Dan took his hands from the wheel and showed his palms to the oncoming road in surrender. 'Ah now Jack, it's only spinning yarns,' he said. 'It's harmless.'

'Was it my fault? Was there any reason in the wide earthly world, so, I'd've done any different?' Jack said, secretly nudging me in the side.

'To shorten the road, isn't that all it is?' I said, returning Jack's nudge.

'We could all sit here like dummies of course. We're all well capable of that,' Dan said.

'Too right, Dan,' I said.

'We all have stories we could tell,' Jack said. 'If we'd a mind to.'

'Forget it so,' Dan said. 'Forget I ever said anything.'

'Go on, he's only narky cause he knows the finish of it,' I said, then turned to Jack. 'Dan now was always smart enough to have a little luck. But you …'

'Would you shut your trap and leave me get on with the story?' Dan said. 'Give someone else a bit of the stage a minute.'

'Was it any of his doing there was no rain the first night?' Jack said.

'Shut your hole you,' I said. 'Go on Dan, you're lying in the bed.'

Up ahead a car was approaching, driving fast, the driver's window down and his elbow out and no headlights in the grey dawn.

'Up I gets anyway and sticks the head out the window,' Dan said.

'The state I'm in, we've nothing better to be listening to?' Jack said.

'Oh Christ I was dying. It was a wonder I didn't cough up

the liver and lamps and all. Up I gets anyway in the morning and the window's clean as a whistle. Grand. A week later it was this fella's turn. I don't know where he got a hold of it, but he was even worse than I'd been, staggering in the door.'

'Only there was no rain,' Jack said. 'End of story, big laugh.'

'Monkey see monkey do, always the way with you,' I said.

As the car came closer I could see two faces in the front and the back was dark but I knew there must have been faces in the back because the driver turned his grey face out of the grey light to say something to the back and then turned his face towards us again.

Dan went on, ignoring the interruption: 'Up the middle of the night he gets, head out the window. This is great he says to himself. Off to school next morning.'

'To the end of my days I've to listen to this shit, just because we'd rain one night and a week later none?'

'When he gets home that evening,' Dan went on, 'Ma was waiting and there was war.'

The driver had taken a long last draw on his cigarette and held it in his fingers and just as they passed us he flicked his fingers and Dan jerked and his words cut off and our car wobbled on the road with Dan brushing his hand frantically at the front of his shirt and glancing up at the road and down at his shirt and up and down until finally he settled himself again. It was a very impressive shot to make at that speed. At the speed they were travelling it would've been a hard enough shot to make if we'd been parked, but to make it when we were travelling towards them at more or less the same speed was very impressive.

Jack had twisted around in his seat and was looking back the way we'd come.

'Bastards,' he said between his teeth, to himself. There was nothing he could say. 'Bastards,' he said again.

'Give us a look?' I said to Dan.

He rubbed the side of his face with the ball of his thumb. 'I'm alright,' he said.

Jack turned around again.

'Jesus Christ Almighty, what country is it we're living in?' he said.

He sat and stared at the road ahead and did a very good impression of a man fuming with rage.

'I'd know them again,' he said after a while. 'I'd know them again.'

The sky was brightening all the time, a cloudless sky. It would be blue when the sun rose but the sun was still behind the mountains and as yet the sky was the dull white of a dirty sheet. There would be frost on the ditches and in the fields that was hard to see now because there were still only grey ditches and fields under a grey sheet. The sun would have to rise higher to bring out the whiteness of the frost against the grass and the briars. As the sun rose, the whiteness of the frost would begin to fade till there was no white left except in the shadows of the ditches, the shadows made black by the whiteness under them and the brightness of the sun on the neighbouring grass. But then the whiteness would fade in the heat of the day unless it was very cold and a wind blew and the frost survived the afternoon and froze over again in the night.

A few miles shy of Naas we swung round a tight bend and had to swerve up onto the grass to avoid running into the back of a Ford. There was no driver to be seen. There was a pony and trap in front of the empty Ford and in front of the trap a knot of seven or eight men standing and smoking and talking and smoking pipes, all of them with rifles over their shoulders and in uniform. Beyond the men were two horseless carts parked sideways on the road, their shafts reared into the air.

'See how we're fixed, will you?' Dan said. I got out and looked at the wheels. The ground was soft but there was plenty of grass under the wheels and the back wheels were only a few feet from the road.

'Try her,' I said. 'I'd say you're grand.' Dan turned his head to Jack and his lips moved and Jack got out of the cab and stood back a few feet with his hands in his pockets and watched the wheels, leaving the door open. Dan put his arm along the back of the seat and looked out the back. The wheels didn't spin. The truck reversed cleanly and smoothly back onto the road and he worked the steering-wheel and swung smoothly into line. The engine was loud in the early dawn. The cab door slammed and Dan came over and stood beside us with his hands in his pockets. Every sound was loud in the quiet country dawn.

One of the men with the rifles hailed us over the roof of the Ford as he and another came down towards us.

'How're the men?' he said, loud and very friendly.

Jack and Dan nodded back in silence. It was still cold and I went over and slammed Jack's door. A jury of crows sat on a leafless ash tree in the ditch with their chins sunk in their chests and making themselves as small as they could, watching us. There were birds stirring in the distance and testing their throats, but the crows made no sound.

'Where ye coming from?' he said, bright and friendly as before. Now they were standing opposite us. Through the space between the Ford and the truck we could see the full length of them and how they were dressed and how they stood. We stood where we were.

'Dublin,' Jack said.

'I thought ye might be alright. And where ye off to this early hour?' he said. I couldn't place his accent. He was talking too brightly and forcing his words. His friend said nothing but he too had on a friendly face and he was smiling and very relaxed in the way he stood. They were both smoking cigarettes and smoking very little of them. They were holding their cigarettes loosely and only occasionally pulling on them and pulling lightly, as if just to keep them alight, smoking like men who have no shortage of cigarettes.

'We're bringing the brother down home, down to Mitchelstown, for to be buried. He died two days ago,' Jack said, with a nod towards the back of the truck.

'Three days ago now,' I said.

'Ye must have been up with the lark,' the soldier said.

It seemed that the louder he spoke the more he had to simplify his words. He was on the far side of the bonnet and he spoke loudly. His voice sounded unfamiliar, as though it were not his own, even though we'd never heard his voice before. It was louder and clearer.

The one who had yet to speak glanced into the cab and then went to take a look in the back of the truck. He looked back at the one with the voice. The one with the voice went to take a look in the back of the truck. He opened the trunk and rearranged its contents and then he looked over to us and then into the back. We stood where we were, as we were.

'I'm sorry lads, but ye'll have to open her up,' the voice said.

We looked at him.

'I'm sorry lads.'

His belt was too tight outside his tunic and he had his thumb hooked inside it and the new leather creaked when he moved his thumb. He needed to punch a new hole in the very tip of the belt. He cleared his throat. He cleared it again, as if something had gone down the wrong way. Each time he cleared it the leather creaked.

Dan stood where he was. Jack looked at Dan and took his hands out of his pockets and went and climbed up on the bed of the truck and undid the ropes. The two men were smoking a lot now. When Jack was finished with the ropes I went over and climbed up beside him and helped him lift off the lid. We stood there high above the two men with the rifles, holding the lid between us. The lid was not so heavy. It was more the size of it and the awkwardness that called for the two of us. The talker lifted his chin, making himself an inch higher, the better to look in, and he tilted forward and then eased himself back onto his heels.

'Thanks lads,' the voice said. 'Sorry about that lads but you know yourself, the way things have been going.'

The other one nodded to me and Jack and then to Dan standing alone on the grass and the two of them walked back to the others at the front, walking in a very relaxed and nonchalant way, but smoking a lot. They pulled the cart on the left up onto the grass and once we were down from retying the ropes they waved us through ahead of the Ford and the trap. We took our time getting back into the truck and let them make an even bigger show of waving us through. All the other men tipped their caps as we passed. I looked for a driver for the Ford or the trap but could see none.

After a while Jack said to Dan: 'Where did you learn to tie a knot?'

Dan didn't answer. Jack got out a packet of cigarettes and put one between his lips and jerked the pack so that a few jutted out and held it out:

'Choose your weapon.'

I took one and put it between my lips. He offered the pack to Dan. Dan's eyes flicked to the pack and then back to the road again and his lips parted slightly. Jack held a cigarette up to the lips and the lips took it. Jack searched himself for matches, finding none. I patted myself down, finding none. Jack made a half-joke of patting Dan down with the flat of his right hand. He had to twist awkwardly to do it. He was particularly thorough about the hips and thighs. Dan put on the face of a disgruntled man.

'Jesus Christ lads,' Dan said, 'have we no light? Between the three of us? See is there a box floating round the floor there some place.'

Jack twisted in another way and put his head between his knees. He really wanted a cigarette. I knew I had a lighter floating around on the floor some place. I'd dropped it there the night before but Jack couldn't find it and I never found it after. It must have been taken later that afternoon, when the truck was taken.

'Jack,' I said, 'there's women for that kind of thing.' Dan did not laugh but he said nothing. All was forgiven. Jack surfaced again and no matches. The three of us sat staring at the road ahead, each with an unlit cigarette between his lips, saying nothing. That was a joke too. There was blue in the sky now.

'Christ I'm hanging for a smoke,' Jack said. 'And a pint to settle my stomach.'

'Are you that bad still?' Dan said.

'I'm alright. Only a pint would do wonders for me.'

'Would you eat?' Dan said.

'I might. But would it stay down, that's the rub.'

Dan shook his head. 'You must be starving. Sure you put nothing solid into yourself since yesterday lunch-time.'

'I'm getting a bit peckish alright,' Jack said.

'Let the record show the word used by the witness was "peckish". Peckish are you, darling? Indeed.'

'We'll pull over now in a bit,' Dan said.

In the fields the sheep lifted their heads from the grass and paused in a reverent stillness and silence to watch us pass. The sheep were fat with wool, long overdue, lying on the grass and standing in groups and here and there one standing apart, all watching us, and between the fields the hedges were skinny and threadbare and grey without leaves. The land was fairly flat and stretched evenly to the horizon, with no hills or mountains bordering it, only the flat straight horizon where the blue of the sky faded to white and the horizon obscured by ditches and broken lines of trees close and far. Where the trees were few and closely gathered in strict geometries and dark green, that was a house. White smoke rose from the dark green trees. Where there was a line of taller elm or ash or lime, that was the drive up to a house. The sun was very low in the sky and melted and stretched the shadows of the ditches and the trees and the houses, stretching them towards the west, where it was not yet so bright. Whenever the road swung to the east the sun was blinding and made everything between us and it either black or white. There was no detail to anything with the sun in our eyes. Whenever the road swung to the east Jack and I dropped our heads and looked up at the world from under our eyebrows. Dan didn't seem to mind.

Early Morning

To our right, quarter of a mile off, a long unending spine raised itself slightly above the level of the fields. It ran straight and true while the road veered gently and gently dipped and rose. In between us and the spine the hedges were sparse and brittle and only just starting to flesh themselves out with leaves, the grey of the stone walls within the hedges still visible, ditches of briar and thorn, just coming into leaf, and on top of the ditches stood the occasional ash and elm still barren and grey and all the while the truck rising and falling as on a gentle swell. We would drop out of sight of the spine but when we rose again there it would be, beyond the freshly ploughed fields and the fields of ruffled grass, inescapable, driving straight and true, indifferent to the landscape, lifted up over hollows and levelling rises like another horizon. Gradually, despite the occasional prevarication, the road sidled up to the track. The track veered gently to the right and we veered with it. There was something on the track up ahead, flickering in and out of sight beyond the ditches. Now the road was running parallel to the track and we were steadily approaching whatever was on the track but not approaching it as fast as we should have been. Whatever was on the track was moving too, moving along the track in the same direction as we, and at a fair pace. A line of ash in-between broke off suddenly and all was revealed. Two boys were working a cabby-car, ferociously. Already, before we were ready, we were up to them. Dan eased off a little and we eased up opposite them and stayed there, the distance between us swelling and shrinking with the run of the road and us bobbing up and down as the road rose and fell and all the while the track running straight and true and perfectly level.

'Keep your eye on the road,' I said.

The boy in front lifted his head and looked over at us and said something to his opposite. It was not so easy for the opposite to look around and keep pumping but he whipped his neck round for an instant to look at us, pumping all the while. Jack rolled the passenger window right down and hefted himself up and sat on the door with only his legs inside.

'What's yer hurry lads?' he shouted.

They kept pumping furiously.

'The cavalry is coming!' Jack shouted. 'The cavalry is coming!' Outside, in the wind and the sound of the engine, his voice sounded far away, but within inches of my head the roof had boomed loud and brittle and hollow and at the first blow I had cringed, without wanting to. He was walloping the roof with his fist again. But now I sat as I was. All I could see were his legs and his waist. He was half out his window and looking back down the line. I twisted myself to see what he saw. A lone engine was moving up the line at an easy pace. It let out two long urgent whistles and then it let out two more, closing in on the boys all the while and slowing gently as it came. The boy in front looked up and put his head down and they pumped. They pumped like toys. Dan let out two blasts of the horn and the engine answered. The engineer stuck his head out the side and gave us a wave and he leaned out further trying to get a look at the boys. He had been able to see them before because of the curve and he knew they were there. On the far side of the engine I could see the legs and waist of the fireman, leaning out too. There was no coal or wood in the tender, that I could see. The toys were tiring but for a few seconds more they held it ten or twelve feet in front of the engine and neither seemed to move and neither seemed to be moving and then the cabby-car seemed to go backwards. The bumper of the cabby-car kissed the bumper of the engine and bounced out and the puppets pumped harder and it closed in gently again and kissed again and stayed kissed. The puppet at the front let go and the handle shot up and just clipped its chin and he jerked back like a puppet and then the strings were cut and it dropped straight to the floor, straight onto its backside. The other one backed off more carefully, knowing how to do it, and sat down. The handles kept pumping maniacally. The boys were not needed anymore. The boy in front was rubbing his chin and a little black line came out of the side of his mouth or it looked black from a distance and in the early morning. The road was running right alongside the line now. The engine raised its tempo and the wheels of the cabby-car were chattering along the line. The boy at the back lay down on his back and let out a long howl and batted his hand over his mouth. He was robbing trains in the Wild West. The engine and the engine of the truck were very loud and the wind torrented past the windows and the redskin was very far away. As Dan shifted the stick the engine paused and then leapt up a fifth and we eased up alongside the engine again.

I twisted round. The coffin was shuddering on the bed of the truck and shuddering hard and fast and frantically. The coffin was in two and three and four places at the one time. We were really travelling now. You could hear it in the engine. There were two and three and four different coffins in the back, all the same, all within an inch of each other, as in a photograph where someone had moved and then stayed. We were going fast but it seemed even faster because we were racing.

'How fast will she go?' I said.

'Ah she's a bit left in her yet,' Dan said.

Now we were opposite the boys. The boy at the front was looking over now. He wiped away the blood with the back of his hand and cupped his hand at his mouth and shouted a few words. He had to shout very loudly, slowly, simply, on account of the engine.

'Dan,' I said quietly, but firmly, because I could see what was coming up ahead and I could see us not making it. But he was listening to the boy, not me.

'WHAT?' Dan roared.

The boy shouted again, the same sounds, even slower and louder.

'Dan,' I said, louder.

'WHAT?' Dan roared.

Under the bonnet, the melody shifted from tenor to alto and we pulled ahead of the cabby-car. A level-crossing sign popped up and was gone.

'We are going to die,' I said confidently.

The boy on his back let out a long howl and stamped his feet on the floor of the cabby-car. We could see it but we could not hear it. Jack was leaning very far out.

The road veered a little away from the line. I could see the crossing three hundred yards up.

The road ahead swerved back again, preparing to cut through the line at a very oblique angle. Dan was in top gear with his foot to the floor.

The two boys were watching us with open mouths. We weren't twenty yards ahead of the engine.

The engineer was smiling. He could have slowed it more but he wanted to play it just right.

The wheels went over the lines with two light thumps so close together they were one thump. We were so close to the boys we could have spat at them. That's how close we were. That's what the engineer understood by just right. The boy had howled again as we passed before them.

After the crossing, the road quickly drew away from the line, much more quickly than it had approached it.

The engine let off two more whistles and Dan answered with the horn. After a while we couldn't see the engine any more, only its smoke and the trail of smoke it had left behind to tell where the line was, the smoke fading in the distance until in the far distance it blended perfectly with the mist that still blurred the air after the night gone by, not yet burnt away by the sun.

The ditches were thick with hawthorn and blackthorn and high with ash, the trees leaning towards each other overhead. The low sun leaked through to us and flickered across the bonnet and into our eyes when we turned towards the east, and then the road would wheel petulantly and the sun which existed only in tatters of sun dangling in the treetops would pass from right to left and out of sight. It was warm in the cab when the sun found us out in the open and cool when it played in our eyes through the trees and when the canopy of trees overhead was untattered it was cold as winter. The windows were still down from shouting at the boys. Jack and Dan rolled up the windows and I got out a cigarette and put it in my mouth.

'We've no fire,' Jack said.

'I know,' I said.

Then there were suddenly no more trees and I realised that there'd been no trees for some time now and that I was sweating. That was the sun and the glass and the heat of the engine and our coats and because it was mid-morning. The fields were sparsely populated with black and brown cows and calves and dust-coloured cows. Off in the distance the farmhouses had nestled into whatever hollows they could find in the flat of the land and surrounded themselves with evergreens. In the fields not yet pastured the grass was unkempt after the winter and there were fields in flood and double lines of elm and ash and beech telling of another long straight road venturing off into the distance resolutely or a long driveway up to a house and light on the water and the wind changing the light.

'This heat has me dead,' Jack said. He opened his overcoat and flapped his shirt and rolled down his window an inch.

'I thought you said you were cold,' Dan said.

'I was. Now I'm hot.'

The wind roared in the gap like a high fire.

'Are we going to have to starve or what before we can eat?' Jack said.

'I want to check the tires anyway,' Dan said. 'These roads. You'd wonder what century you were in.'

We drove on for another mile and then he eased up onto the grass by a gateway and we got out. There were gate-posts but no gate and they'd dragged a few furze bushes into the gap against the cattle wandering. Right by this, there was a telegraph pole lying on the ground. Jack went over.

'Jack,' I said.

'What?' he said, sitting down.

'The tar on that.'

He considered the pole under him and dabbed at it with a finger and stood up again and turned his back to me.

'A hit, a very palpable hit!' I declared.

He patted his arse with his palm and then studied the palm.

'A pox on't!' he said.

Dan walked around the truck with his head tilted to one side like a coy girl, kicking the tires with his toe, expertly. He went to the back and let down the flap of the truck and sat up on the bed with one of the newspapered parcels and a bottle of tea beside him and I went over and sat on the other side. Jack came over with his head craned round to look at his arse and pulling the seat of his pants round to the front. He stood facing us.

'Now, let's see what the Legion think we deserve,' Dan said.

Inside the newspaper there were sandwiches wrapped in butcher-paper. There were cheese and ham, the slices of cheese and ham thick and tough to chew and your jaw was tired chewing after two or three. The bread was good batch loaf and after two or three you felt like you had eaten. We took a good bite and drank and passed the bottle. The tea was very strong, a lot of tea-leaves in the bottom and we drank and passed it gently, trying not to stir them up. Sooner or later one of us would get a mouthful but we went on drinking, less and less as we neared the end, none of us wanting to be the one.

There were brown and black calves in the field, the field rushy and marshy at the far side and with clumps of furze and long-dead grass from the winter the colour of straw and the new grass underneath showing through fresh and green. The calves came over from the shelter of a thorn ditch and looked at us through the furze. Outside the cab there was very little heat from the sun. There was a light wind and clouds moved across the sun and it was like winter without the sun and we didn't stay sitting long. The wood of the bed was cold under us at first and never really warmed up. Jack didn't sit at all but stamped up and down before us, one hand under his armpit and feeding himself with the other and taking his hand out from under his armpit when it was his turn for the bottle.

'Could we not have it in the truck? he said.

'We're finished now anyway,' Dan said.

When we were finished Dan and I balled up the newspaper and the butcher-paper and brought them back to the trunk with the bottle, for lighting the fire later.

'Stall,' Jack said, and followed us round and rummaged in the trunk amongst the papers we'd wedged there. He took out a ball of newspaper and opened it out. *The Evening Star.* Kate's, presumably. 'That rag,' Jack said, flinging it back in, 'I wouldn't even do it the courtesy. And don't give me *The Times* either, that'd cut the arse right out of you.'

The next ball was acceptable to him and he walked off round the truck, over to the furze. As he kicked a gap in the furze, the calves scampered away lanky and awkward and unfamiliar with their legs. Dan and I turned and sat on the back again to wait, trying not to hear what we heard from inside the ditch, but twice or three times we couldn't help but look at each other in dismay. After a few minutes we heard the gate swinging open again and Jack came strolling out, buckling his belt.

'Well whatever he puts in it, that bastard Clancy,' he said, 'it comes out pure black.'

Morning

There were still patches of white in the shadows of the ditches, the white very white in the blackness and the black blackened by the bright sun on the neighbouring grass. Up ahead, the roadside ditches veered to and fro, the distance drawing them together till far off there seemed only to be one ditch and then further off again there was only the line of telegraph poles, some at strict attention, some tilting towards each other the way headstones do. That was the road ahead. We had an hour of clear driving, meeting very little traffic, before we met the next checkpoint, well out of Naas. A Crossley tender was parked sideways across the road. That was the roadblock. A black tourer had just been let through and there were no other cars. Two cars came from the other direction as we approached and they waved them straight through but both slowed to a snail's pace until they were well clear on our side. Dan saw he could drive straight up to it and kept his speed up and the men all turned and at the last moment Dan braked hard and stopped the truck right up to within a foot of the foremost of them, who stood in a defiant and heroic pose in the middle of the road, his rifle at half-mast. He slung the rifle onto his shoulder and came round to the driver's door and spat and looked in the open window at the three of us.

'Where ye coming from, comrades?' he said, his voice dry and chopped. He wasn't happy about Dan's little game.

'Das Capital, comrade,' I said.

'Out,' he said.

I looked at Jack and Jack looked at Dan and then back at me. Dan was staring straight ahead. The man stepped back from the truck and swung his rifle off his shoulder and held it with the stock low on his right thigh and the barrel across his chest up to his left shoulder. I'd like to have seen him pull the trigger and see what it did to his leg.

'Swear to God ...' he said.

'Swear to God!' Jack hissed to me. 'He invokes heaven 'gainst me! I am quite turned to jelly.'

'Now!' He was shouting now.

'Will we hear ourselves treated so?' Jack implored.

'Stay brother!' I urged him. 'Now's not the time.'

'Fie! 'Tis the time when 'tis heard!' shouted Jack, or almost shouting.

Outside the cab we heard the clean, honest action of the rifle's machinery, as he drew back the bolt. Letting the engine idle, Dan very casually stepped out onto the road, leaving the cab door open and he stood on the road with his hands in his pockets.

'O were my wishes more than words!' Jack whimpered. 'There's some would ne'er again ope their mouths but howl.'

I got out and Jack slid over and got out my door and strolled round and stood beside me at the front of the truck so that the man with the rifle was between us and Dan. He didn't appreciate that either. Dan took a step or two further away so that the man couldn't see all three of us at once. He backed off immediately and nodded to the two of us to go over to where Dan was. Jack strolled over and I took a step and stopped and took out a cigarette and put it between my lips and patted myself down and lifted my head and with the cigarette between my lips asked the rifle had he a light. He just looked at me, unsure of how he should look at me. I turned to the other men standing a few yards off and asked them and one of them threw over a box of matches. I lit the cigarette very carefully, checking more than once that it was properly lit. In the field adjacent, rooks were laughing and wheeling about a tall elm.

'Get over there,' the man said.

I lobbed the box back and got over there. The rifle turned his head to the others.

'Johnny keep an eye on this crowd here,' he said.

'Has heaven not an ear?' Jack moaned to me, quietly. 'Is there no lightening left, or is't stocked up for heavier vengeance?'

'Peace, quench thy zeal, brother,' I beseeched him, ''tis dangerous to thy bosom.'

'Pardon, brother,' he relented, 'and prithee do not weigh me by my passions.'

I laid a forgiving hand on his shoulder: 'I ne'er weighed brother so, brother.'

Jack made a point of looking about to see if we were the only ones. We were the only ones.

A fair-haired boy who looked no more than fourteen with baggy sleeves and rolled-up cuffs came over and took the rifle from him. The rifle was too big for him too. He held it very stiffly, with the stock cradled in his belly and the barrel at a perfect right angle to his body. I'd like to have seen him pull the trigger and see what it did to his breakfast. The first one looked in the side window into the cab and then stepped back to the trunk and opened that. He went back to the cab and when he'd searched everywhere and left everything as untidy as he possibly could, he walked down the far side of the truck and let down the back flap and considered the contents with an expert eye. Two others followed him, less certain of themselves. He dropped his head and said something into his shoulder and one of them climbed up onto the bed of the truck. The first one reached inside his jacket and drew out a large skinning-knife and held it pinched at the nib and flicked his hand effetely. The man standing up on the truck jerked his feet backwards and the back of his legs met a rope and he teetered a moment off-balance and wheeled his arms as though he would fall backwards right out of the truck. The knife hit the bed of the truck with a single clean note. I heard it but I could not see it for the sides. The men laughed without enthusiasm. The man in the truck bent down and came back up with the knife in his hand. Blade up, he put the knife under the rope and in a single smooth motion drew it towards himself, obliquely, drawing the edge along the underside of the rope. He did that four times and each time the two new ends of the rope whipped back away from the blade. Dan had tied everything tight. The first one dropped his head again and said something else into his shoulder and another one of them got up onto the bed of the truck. The boy with the rifle who was supposed to be watching us was watching them through the windscreen and the back window and the rifle had dropped to an angle of about forty-five degrees with the ground. Forty-five or anything less was fine by me. The two men stood on the same side and lifted up that side of the lid and flicked it hard. I listened to it clatter onto the bed of the truck. The two of them stood up straight with their backs to us and looked in and then they looked at the first man. He was smoking the last half-inch of a butt and pinched it and held it away from himself to look at it and took a last drag and parted his fingers and let it drop between his feet and looked at it again where it lay on the ground and ground it with his sole. He lifted his leg up into the bed of the truck, and gripped and shifted his weight and gripped again, struggling to get up. One of his men came up behind him to help but he flapped him away extravagantly. We watched him trying to get up onto the truck. Eventually he got up onto the truck.

He looked in and then he bent over and supported himself with one hand and put the other hand inside, feeling all the way around the sides with the two men beside him standing with their backs to us and their hands in their pockets looking down. When he was done he stood and stepped to the edge and sat down and very awkwardly eased himself off the edge and dropped down onto the ground. He was slow standing up fully straight again. The other two jumped off bravely and landed cleanly, each hitting the ground with a neat, coy sigh. The boy lifted the rifle from forty-five to ninety again and looked at us fiercely, his feet wide apart and his mouth tight and looking at us from under his eyebrows, whoever that was supposed to be. The first man came back and took his rifle and looked at us and jerked his head.

'Alright,' he said. 'And wipe that smile off your face you. Before I do it for you.'

We watched him go. When they were all gone, Jack turned and asked us frankly:

'Would the knave have me occupy the world as I entered it, complaining?'

Dan turned away from us and went down the back and climbed up and fixed the lid and started to work the ropes. Jack sighed and went back to help him. Dan had undone one end of each rope, left out some slack and tied the end again, to then tie the two severed ends as best they could. It was an utterly idiotic way of going about things, but I said nothing. Because of where they'd cut them, none of the severed ends would be long enough in itself. They could have cut them close to the end and we would have been able to let out some slack and use them as they were. It was Jack's job to hold the two ends tight while Dan worked the very ends into a knot, trying to tie them in such a way that none of the tension was lost in pulling the knot tight. Instead of leaving the end proper untied, tying the two severed ends together, and then tying the end proper as normal again. But I said nothing, and watched. Apart from the basic strategy, Dan knew what he was doing, but if Jack wasn't keeping up the tension he was wasting his time, and he left Jack in no doubt about this. Jack did his best but on the third knot I could see him sweating again and on the fourth his arms started to shiver with the strain. That was how tight it all had to be, doing it this way. Dan was very slow and deliberate with his work and totally taken with the rope and it was ten minutes before we were ready.

Only when we were all three in the cab and were gunning the engine did they even begin to move their own truck out of the way. They turned it very meticulously, making sure the wheels did not go up into the grass.

Driving, Dan's lips were closed tight and his eyes were unblinking and fixed on the rear-view mirror.

'Keep your eyes on the road,' I said.

Eventually Dan said: 'I'm going to say this once and I'm not going to say it twice. Ye want to go and give them the excuse they're looking for, sure as fuck they'll make shit of ye and maybe ye don't give a shit but I'm telling ye this now, ye think they'll leave me stand on the ditch for to watch? My bollocks.

So we keep our mouths shut and our hands in our pockets and we'll be in Cork by the morning. In one piece. Maybe. Anything else, I don't want to hear it.'

That was his speech, however long he'd been rehearsing it.

There were fields of grass to each side and traces of cart-wheels through the grass and ash trees growing on the ditches, the ditches barren beneath the dead briars, the dead briars the colour of straw and the ash trees stark and grey like dead trees and where there were walls under the briars the walls smoothed over with earth and grass. A lone horse stood picking very particularly at what was growing on a ditch, beyond it an old broken stone house in the middle of the field, fenced off, used as a corral for cattle.

'Big fucking men they are alright with their guns in their fists,' Jack said. 'Give me two minutes inside a ditch, Sweet Jesus how I wouldn't rearrange them.'

'What am I after saying to you?' Dan said.

'Their mothers wouldn't know them,' Jack said.

'What am I after saying to you?' Dan said.

'Don't worry about me. I can take care of myself.'

'What am I after saying to you Jack?'

Jack did not answer. Dan went on staring out the windscreen. I watched his fingers and how they gripped the wheel and how he changed the gears and listened to how he worked the engine and remembering how he had worked it before.

The road veered slowly to the left and up ahead on the right was a large farmhouse with a lawn sloping up to it from the road. There had been frost the last few nights and someone had crossed the lawn in the night and broken the frozen grass and already the grass was black where it had been broken and died and now a line of lone black footprints led across the grass, leading up to the door of the house.

'So what plans have you for the shop?' I asked Jack.

'You mean will I hang on to it?'

'Well it's that or sell it.'

'I don't know. It was just something to get him out of bed in the morning the last few years. Sure he was biting at a bare hook for years with it, far as I can see. Sure you saw it yourself, the state of the place.'

'Why don't you just sell it so?'

'If someone would buy it,' Jack said.

'And what kind of price are we talking?'

He dropped his head, thinking about what I had said, or at least he seemed to be thinking about it, or about something, or at least he fell silent and dropped his head and his forehead wrinkled where it had not been wrinkled before and he remained quiet for a while, frowning like a man deep in thought or like a man trying to work a bit of food out from a back tooth. I waited. But he didn't know or he wouldn't say or he hadn't heard my question. In any case he said nothing and we drove on without talking.

'Do you want us to take the wheel a bit?' I said to Dan.

'I'm grand.'

'Well give us a shout when you want a break.'

'I said I'm grand,' said Dan. 'Sure we've been stopped more than we've been going nearly.'

The road beyond Naas was not the best. The seat was of red leather and the leather was tight and packed hard and very little give in it. With the back all but empty the suspension was high and the backs of those trucks bounced around a lot when they weren't carrying much weight. That was always the one big drawback with those trucks. The books wouldn't have made much difference. We'd have needed too many of them, with no room in the box itself, so that on top of everything else we'd have had to worry about giving them a box of their own and tying that down and keeping it tied and all the rest of it. The suspension in the front was alright but with the back jumping around a lot and so little give in the seat we were being bounced about a lot. It was that or slow down even more and as it was the roads had been getting progressively worse and we were no longer making such good time. In the bright of the day you could see the state of the road up ahead and brace with your legs and after a while you were tired from bracing yourself and holding yourself tight all the time. When the evening came on you couldn't see so far ahead or so clearly and you didn't brace yourself all the time but it was only coming up to noon and the evening was a long way away yet.

'And what about Kate?' I asked. 'If you decide to sell.'

No one answered. We were talking less loudly now because the engine seemed quieter in the brightness. In the darkness and for some time afterwards I had imagined that the engine could be heard for miles around. Maybe it could. But it did not seem so loud now. I repeated the question.

'Look, have we to talk about this right here and now?' Dan said.

I looked at him. He had the same face as always, obsessed with the road ahead.

'We've got to sort it out sometime,' I said. 'You know as well as I do.'

'I know we do, but has it to be right here and now, has it?'

'Of course not,' I said. 'Maybe we'll organise a colloquium on the subject. For, say, autumn twelve months, when you've finished your lecture tour. How would that suit you? Or do you have to check your diary?'

Dan said nothing to this.

'I think I could probably pencil you in,' Jack said brightly.

I looked to Dan for a response, a reaction of some sort.

'Fine,' I said.

In the ditches alongside the road you could tell where there was a wall because of the solid bank of ivy under the briars.

'So tell us, what's it like over on the other side?' Jack said after a while.

'I suppose it's alright,' I said. 'It's Liverpool, it's like Liverpool. I don't know.'

'The witness will please answer the question,' Jack said.

'Jesus Christ,' Dan said, 'the Spanish Inquisition.'

'It's like the quays only the porter is piss and the women aren't complete and utter … That's what it's like. The quays in November,' I said.

'Oh it's the women now is it?' Jack said. 'Well God in heaven, how willingly youth is corrupted. And tell us now, have they figured out how to work a contraption the like of you yet, these daughters of Albion, these damsels bright, these visions of delight, these radiant sisters of the night?' There was rapture in his voice. 'And tell us where dwell the joys of old, and where the ancient loves? And when will they renew again the night of oblivion past?'

'Your honour,' I said, 'must my client tolerate this line of questioning?'

'Go on,' Jack said, 'you know we're all friends here. It won't go beyond these four walls.'

I looked at him down the length of my nose, eyebrows raised.

'Go on you dirty Arab.'

'Objection!' I said.

He drew back his elbow and his fist as if to throw a punch. I mirrored this. We feinted and bobbed and weaved our heads. I was beside Dan and every time I pulled back I knocked into him and the truck flirted with its true course. I had Jack's head under my arm and I was punching him dully in the back of the neck and he was pushing forwards trying to break my grip. His face was all but on Dan's lap.

'Lads! Lads!' Dan shouted, 'would ye cop the fuck on with yerselves would ye!'

'Order! Order!' I roared, banging the base of my fist on Jack's back. 'If there is another display of that kind I shall have the gallery cleared!'

I let him up. He rubbed the flat of his palms back and forth across his ears and scrunched up his face in mock indignation.

'Motion to have the hearing deferred?' I inquired. Jack gave me that look of daring he'd had when drawing back his fist first. 'Motion granted!' I said, and slammed the dash. 'Now the next case before the court, I believe, is a petition brought by Lady Pilkington-Langford seeking to dissolve her marriage with Lord Pilkington-Langford, on the grounds of non-consummation. The petitioner herself, I understand, is to be examined first. In you go, counsel.'

'Ye're a pair of fucking messers, the pair of ye,' Dan said.

'Indeed sir,' Jack said grandly, extending his hand across me. 'Messers Exham and Clarke, formerly of the Inner Temple. I don't believe we've had the pleasure.'

'Go on,' Dan said, 'and don't be acting the maggot.'

Jack rubbed the flat of his palms across his ears again. 'You brute,' he said in a delicate voice, batting his eyelashes, 'I never wish to set eyes on you again.'

'Gimme a fag before I bate ye, the pair of ye,' Dan said.

'It's his way of saying he loves you,' Jack confided in me.

'Oh Dan, *macushla*, did you miss me? Why, I never suspected. Why on earth didn't you say something? Some little sign …'

'Why he never talked about anything else,' Jack said, 'all

the time you were away. Why, he said, if I must fall then it is for the love of that Gael I shall fall. Splendid and holy causes are served by men who are themselves splendid and holy, splendid in the proud manhood of him, splendid in the Gaelic strength and the simplicity of devotion and the clarity and the truth of him.'

'I swear ...' said Dan through his teeth, and raised his hand in threat, though I was the only one close enough.

Jack laughed, glad to have elicited even that reaction.

Dan sat with the cold cigarette still between his lips. 'Mother of fuck lads have we still no light?' He snapped away the cigarette and flung it at the dash.

The seat under us was tight and hard and the truck was bouncing along the road and there was very little give in the seat. The back was high, being all but empty, and very light and bouncing around a lot on account of how little weight it was carrying, the way those trucks did. The suspension in the front was good but the back was jumping all over the place with the state of the road and we on the hard seat were jumping with it. The sun was behind a bank of cloud and we had rolled up the windows again and the truck was old and the cab smelled of cigarettes and smoke and oil and petrol and stale drink and I could see Jack's hands gripping his thighs.

'How's the head now?'

'It's not the head I'm worried about.'

'If you want to stop now,' Dan said.

'I'm bursting anyway,' I said.

'There's a village not too far now,' Dan said. 'I have to go myself.'

'I'd murder a pint,' Jack said.

'Tell us something we don't know,' I said.

'Is there some place we can get a drink?'

Dan looked at him with incredulity. 'Would you listen to

him, Lawrence of Arabia. I want to check the ropes anyway, after those bad bastards.'

'Who'll watch the truck,' I said and instantly wished I had not said it.

'Jesus Christ,' Dan said, 'I know times are tough, but for fuck sake, we're not out of Connaught yet.'

'Is this it here?' Jack said, nodding at a house up ahead, on the far side of a crossroads.

'It is, if I remember right,' said Dan.

'Christ I'm bursting,' I said.

Dan shifted down through the gears, slowing the truck almost to a crawl.

'Always the life of the party,' I said.

Happy, he picked up the pace again and we paused at the junction and twenty yards on we eased onto a shoulder of gravel beside the pub.

Noon

The house stood alone, right on the road, with a row of palm trees to the rear of it and beyond that a freshly ploughed field. From a distance there was no sign that it was anything other than a private house and then coming closer there were the double doors with glass-panels. There was a dull murmur of voices from within and beyond the glass figures blurred and reshaped by the thick bevelled glass. As we got out of the cab one of the doors swung open and a long thin man in an oilskin squeezed out and as he did so the murmur swelled and resolved itself into distinct voices, the door clapped shut and the voices jellied again. He paused to fit on his cap and considered us as he lifted his head under his cap and then moved off along the road, too heavy and too steady on his feet, like a badly beaten fighter. When he was gone about twenty yards a mongrel sheep-dog trotted out from the blind side of the house and fell in beside him.

The six glass-panels were obviously much older than the door which held them. They were a thicker, less flawless kind of glass than they should have been, for that door, with the quiet currents of their firing still coursing through them, and better crafted, bevelled and each of the six etched with a mythological figure. It was not so much that they'd been transferred from elsewhere, though there was that too, but that in the transfer the set of six had remained perfectly intact, without so much as a crack or a chip.

I had gone over to look at the glass and I was first in. As I stepped through the door I couldn't help but look about to see how the faces received our entry. This was giving the game away from the start. Most of the men looked around and ceased to speak as they did so, which caused those who had not looked around or ceased to speak to do so now. They considered us with silent and solemn genius. Dan and Jack were standing behind me in the doorway.

'Were you born in a barn were you?' said a man loudly from the near end of the bar.

Dan stepped away from the door and it clapped shut of its own accord. The bar was dim and narrow and long, most of the men standing at the counter, and most still wearing their caps and overcoats. There was a lot of smoke and a strong smell of smoke. The zinc counter turned in at both ends, leaving a small area at the front and the end of the long room where men were seated at small tables. But most of the men were congregated at the bar. There were three or four dogs slinking about between the men's legs, tracking each other and petitioning the men for attention. I nodded at a table nearby as I made my way to the bar. The general murmur had already resumed. The barman was waiting.

Dan spoke over our heads: 'Two pints and a pint of cider if you have it.' He looked at Jack down the length of his nose: 'Think you can keep a pint down?'

'We can but try,' Jack said.

'Cider,' I said. 'Back to the faith of your childhood, is it?'

'Ah the pints haven't been agreeing with me lately,' Dan said.

We unbuttoned our coats and pushed them back over our hips and stood with our hands in our trouser pockets. There were men coming and going all the time, but the space around us was not filled.

Behind the bar, instead of the usual dresser, was a titanic piece of oak shelving, lovingly-carved, all scrolls and vine-leaves and grapes and acanthus leaves, decorative carvings wherever there was room for them. It ran right the length of the bar and from floor to ceiling, so well put together that it all seemed of a piece. The wood was dark and heavy and finely-grained. Later, I'd hear it had been washed up on the coast of Wexford, from the bar of such-and-such a steamer, wrecked in such-and-such a year, with so many lost. How they carted it so far inland I don't know. But even now I could see they'd gone to the trouble of carting it some distance, from some Big House I supposed, making the zinc bar to measure, reassembling it all piece by piece, and then sawing off the top foot of it to fit it under the ceiling.

The drinks arrived eventually.

'That's the last of the cider there now if that's alright for you,' the barman said. The pint glass was about three-quarters full, a yellow liquid topped with a thin, soapy froth. It looked like piss the morning after.

'You know now that's last year's,' I said to Dan.

'What of it?' Dan said.

A pig-farmer came up to the bar. I smelled him coming, bringing a whole world with him.

'Down from Dublin are ye?' he said.

'That's right,' Dan said.

The pig-farmer considered the glass of piss on the counter.

'That's grand,' Dan said to the barman, putting money on the counter.

'The Lote tree of Islam ...' I said, fondly considering the cider, 'the Persian Haoma ... the Kien-mou of China, bounding paradise ... What religion is there for which the tree does not serve as a symbol of renewal? The roots of the tree penetrate the Great Earth Mother and in return, like mother's milk, she gives up her sacred sap in spring, the tree flourishes and in the autumn bears fruit, infused with this elixir of the eternal youth ...'

'Good luck,' Dan said curtly, and he closed his eyes and poured a third of his drink down his throat.

'Speaking of sacred sap, where's the jacks here?' I asked. The pig-farmer's head tilted towards the far end of the bar. I could see a man coming out of a low doorway.

When I got back the pig-farmer was gone.

'Have ye rid ye then o' the pander, brothers?' I inquired. 'How is he now?'

'None the better for your asking,' Jack replied dolefully. 'Your kindest office is to pray for him.'

'Gone none too soon then,' I declared. ''Sfoot, but the knave was familiar as an ague. But tell me quick, noticed not this company his destruction?'

'Ay,' Jack narrated, 'but 'twas so finely managed that the fault was laid at the door of the inn. He had but put his lips to his glass when he cried "Oh! Oh! I am poisoned!"'

'Most craftily done,' I congratulated him. 'But looks it not awry, this absence of any outward grief at our late companion's passing? 'Twould be winning flattery if we couldst wring out a little salt-water. Think of some dame, brother—'twill teach thee to dissemble.'

At this, Jack fell into profound thought.

'Our sorrows are so fluent,' I said, laying a comforting hand upon Dan's shoulder, 'that our eyes o'erflow our tongues. Words spoke in tears are like the murmurs of the waters, the sound is loudly heard, but cannot be distinguished. But how died he, pray?'

'O, full of rage and spleen.'

'He died most valiantly then.'

Dan turned to look around the bar, drawing his shoulder out from under my hand.

Suddenly Jack's eyes widened in terror, looking over my shoulder.

'Alive!' he croaked.

I turned to see what he saw. The pig-farmer was approaching, on his way to the toilet.

'In health!' I proclaimed.

But passing, his silence was his only acknowledgement.

'O hell unto my soul!' I cried.

'O death and vengeance!'

'Hell and torments!'

'O too, too far you have cursed,' Jack muttered to himself. 'Be thy rash tongue the cause of all ensuing harm ...'

'Nigget,' I chided, ''tis only that our confidence was outstripped by our wit.'

'But surely it can be reversed?' Jack returned, speaking into his glass, trying to contain a grin.

'Innkeeper!' I shouted.

Dan shook his head in despair. 'Ye'll break the melt on me the pair of ye,' he said.

The barman came down, disconsolate.

I thumbed my glass: 'Seriously lads, will ye let this cup pass?'

Jack considered his glass and what was left in it. 'Thy will be done,' he said.

'What are you having?' I asked Dan.

'You've no more of this,' he said to the barman, holding up his empty glass.

'That's the last of it there now.'

'Will you have a drop? You will. Whiskey,' I said to the barman, 'and a lump of ice.'

The barman looked at me blankly.

'Whiskey and a drop of water,' Dan said.

'And two pints?' the barman said.

I looked at Jack. He grimaced.

'And two pints,' I said.

The barman went away.

'How do you feel after that now?' Dan asked Jack.

'A bit better.'

'You have to know when to stop,' Dan said.

'Yes, father.'

A man came into the bar, his cap pulled low over his eyes. He came up to the counter close to us and ordered a drink. He had to raise his head a little so that the barman would hear him. His face was very bruised and very swollen, both eyes almost closed. The nose had been broken recently and not reset. It was black beneath the skin at the top of the bridge. The lips were all puffed up and all scabs, as if the teeth had gone through them. When he ordered his drink he only opened a little gap at the corner of his mouth and later when he drank he would hold the glass to that side and try as best he could to pour the drink in that gap, pushing his head back as far as he could. Even before beginning to drink he would have his handkerchief out to wipe himself. His fingers were black under the skin. He would drink slowly and deliberately, holding the cloth at his chin under the glass so that none of it would run down onto his shirt. The scabs were drying out and at the edges they were starting to come away from the new skin underneath. Waiting for his drink to come, he kept his eyes fixed on the row of bottles inside the bar.

It must have been a terrible beating. He took a cigarette out of his inside pocket and put it in the gap and felt in his pocket. A neighbour immediately produced a lit match and he turned his back to us and bowed his head as if asking for blessing and the other one brought up his hand as if to make the sign of the cross on the battered forehead and he lifted up his head and nodded in acknowledgement and turned his eyes back to the bottles. That's what I thought it looked like at the time. After a while the barman brought his drink and leaned over with one hand on the counter and pushed the drink in front of him. The man put his hand in his pocket for money and the barman took his hand off the counter and looked up the bar and looked back at the face. The face looked up the bar and nodded and he took up his drink and showed it to whoever was at the end of the bar. After a while he went for a piss. His was the only place free at the bar now and the bar full and men coming and going all the time but no one took his place. His cigarette lay at the edge of the counter, the smoke sending up an unbroken signal, the tip projecting out over the edge of the zinc. When he returned the cigarette was no longer smouldering and a withered half inch of ash hung at the end, a reminder of what had been. He didn't bother to tap it. He didn't have to. As his fingers took hold of it again it just fell away cleanly.

One of the men from a table near the door came up and ordered a round of drinks. He turned a shoulder to us and took a wad of notes out of his pocket and held them low and close to his body and peeled off a lone note in the lee of the counter as discreetly as he could and held it in his hand, waiting for his drinks to come. When his drinks came he would throw the note up on the counter ostentatiously. I looked at the wad and looked at his boots. I don't know why I looked at his boots. They were poor man's boots. Turning, he caught my eye.

'Down from Dublin are ye?' he said.

'Christ,' I said, 'is it that obvious?'

'Ah,' he said, 'they don't miss much round here.'

'Obviously not,' I said.

Jack tugged at my sleeve and hissed in my ear: 'Prithee brother, what counsel would the knave have with thee?'

'He would have news of the court, brother,' I said to Jack, by way of introduction.

'O to think upon the pleasure of the palace,' Jack mused. 'Securéd ease and state ... banquets abroad by torch-light ... finest silks ...'

'We're in disguise,' I confided, acknowledging our apparel.

'... music ... maidens ... sports ...'

The local smiled uncertainly: 'The women is it?'

'Ah,' I said, turning to Jack, 'this is the man now you want to talk to about that.'

'It's a lie,' Jack said indignantly. 'It's a damned lie and I don't mind telling you so,' and with this he turned brusquely towards the toilet with his drink in his hand, froze, wheeled about glamorously, set his glass down on the bar, then resumed his course.

'You'll have to forgive him,' I said confidentially to our new friend, 'his nerves are all shot to hell since the war. Terrible thing. Lost some damn fine chaps in that scrap.'

'There was plenty round here never came back out of it,' the local said.

I looked at his face.

'Second Royals,' he said.

I wished I'd not said what I'd said.

'Fucking bad business,' Dan said.

The local's round came and he lifted three pints in his giant farmer's hands and turned to go.

'Gentlemen,' he said and moved off stealthily.

In silence, Dan and I watched him negotiate his way through the crowd to his table. A man beside us looked over, looking us up and down, resettled his cap on his head and left the bar, leaving a full half a pint behind him on the bar.

Jack came back. Dan looked at him, waiting to make eye-contact.

'Ah we were only acting the bollix,' Jack said.

About half way through our second drink three or four dogs started to bark outside and then the dogs inside with us began barking. An older man got up from the table nearest the door, drink in hand, leaving his coat on his chair, and held the door open for the dogs to go out and then followed them out. His neighbour rose and did something to the top of the door so that it stayed open and followed the first man out. They stood just off the doorstep, so that we could see them through the open door, looking off to the left, to the junction, where we could not see. The barking from outside was louder now, as though even more dogs had come out of the woodwork. A few of the younger men got up in a hurry and strode out, looking at each other eagerly, and they too looked off to the left and every once in a while threw a glance back inside the bar. More and more men got up and went and joined them outside and they looked too, until eventually there were only seven or eight men left inside, including us, all of us quiet except one pair at the far end of the bar who kept talking in a deliberately casual way. It was impossible to see what those outside saw, off up the junction. All we could see were their faces. The dogs were not barking as much any more. The men had their hands on the dogs, calming them. Except for the pair who'd decided to keep talking, there was almost no sound from within to challenge the murmurs and the sizzle of gravel outside, and then as though the voices had won out even that died, giving way to a sound I knew was the sound of marching, a sound that came out of nowhere and then seemed like it had always been there and then it swelled up a little and just hung there a while, filling the air as though the air were made for that sound and that sound only and after a while it ebbed away again a lot faster than it had come. When it was gone it was quiet again, but the quiet was different from what it had been before. It wasn't parade-ground marching, it wasn't crisp and well-orchestrated marching with the clean crunch of gravel and snare-like, but messy. Maybe it was the dirt road and they were tired or not perfectly trained or maybe they only march like that on the parade-ground. I've always been disappointed by marching not done on the parade-ground. When it was quiet again one man came back in and then they all filed back in and started talking again. A lot had finished their drinks outside and it was two and three deep at the bar for a while and then things were more or less as they had been before.

All the space at the bar was taken except for the space around us.

Dan knocked back the last of his whiskey. 'Ye right?' he said.

Jack and I considered our drinks. There was about a third left in mine and a bit more in his. We knocked them back and Dan nodded to the barman. As we went out, I tried to catch the eye of the local at the table by the door, to nod to him, but he kept his head down and kept talking.

We stepped out onto the gravel and tried to blink away the brightness. The coffin was lying on the gravel.

'I don't believe it,' Dan said.

We stood and shielded our eyes from the sun and looked off into the distance, looking four ways from the crossroads off into the distance and into the brightness.

'I don't believe it,' Dan said. He was staring at the coffin where it lay.

A man on a bicycle came free-wheeling through the cross-roads and hissed up onto the gravel. He stood straddling the cross-bar and looked at us and looked at the coffin. His eyes met mine.

'They're after taking our truck,' I said.

He looked at the coffin.

'And leaving that,' I said.

He looked at the coffin again. There were no tyre-marks in the gravel about the coffin, neither of our coming nor of the truck going.

'It was in the back of the truck?'

'It was.'

He looked at the coffin again.

'Are they only this minute after taking it?'

'We're only just after coming out from inside.'

'Stall a minute there,' he said. He leaned his bicycle up against the wall and went in through the double door.

'I don't believe it,' Dan said.

He came out with the barman and a few more followed them out, drinks in hand. They looked at us and the coffin on the gravel. More came out.

'This man tells me ye're after losing something?' said the barman, saying it as though this was hard to believe.

There was laughter from the back.

'Have yez no homes to go to?' someone shouted.

The man with the bicycle turned around to look at the laughers. 'I think this is gone a bit beyond a joke now Harry,' he said.

'Is that right?' said one of the crowd. 'But sure these lads here love a bit of a joke, don't ye lads?'

Jack went round the side of the house and came back and

looked at Dan and jerked his head towards where he had been. 'Have you the keys?' he said.

Dan went round the back and there was the clean slam of a door and then the engine starting. More laughter backstage. The truck backed around the corner of the house quickly, the wheels spitting gravel, and he backed it up into the road away from the crowd. Just then a Vulcan came through the crossroads and eased up and waited in the middle of the road, its engine idling. Dan came over and we three bent to lift the coffin and the man with the bicycle stepped over and eased his shoulder under it and we shuffled across the gravel and bent our knees and slid it along the back of the truck, listening to the wood grind on the dirt there.

'Thanks,' Jack said.

Dan climbed up onto the bed of the truck to fix the ropes. The man with the bicycle stood near the truck and watched Dan working the ropes.

'Thanks,' I said.

Seeing no prospect of movement, the Vulcan swung up onto the gravel and past us onto the road again, its tracks slicing through the tracks of our feet.

We waited until Dan was finished with the ropes and then we all got in together.

'Some one of ye's after stepping in it,' Jack said instantly.

I breathed in through my nose. 'Jesus fuck,' I said.

Dan moved his knees apart and tilted the soles of his boots up from the floor and looked down at them. 'Not me,' he said.

'Not me.'

'I don't fucking believe it,' Jack said, looking between his feet and looking away. 'They're after shitting on the floor.'

We got out of the truck quickly, leaving the doors open. The crowd erupted into loud and jubilant laughter. We would not look at them. Dan and I went round to where Jack was, with the truck between us and the others. We would not look at each other. I looked into the cab and looked away. It wasn't even as if they'd got the dogs to do it. Jack went round and opened the trunk and brought out some of the newspaper that had wrapped the sandwiches and came back and leaned inside the cab. I did not look. I did not want to close my eyes but I didn't know where to look. Jack stood up straight again and flung the balled-up newspaper over the back of the truck towards the crowd. It flew straight for a few yards and then puffed up suddenly and stalled and hung in the air and dropped dead to the ground like a dead grouse, not even half-way across the gravel. More laughter. We got back into the truck. There was newspaper on the floor under Jack's feet and his feet rustled when they moved. He had his feet wide apart, at the edges of the newspaper. We waited until we were out of sight before rolling down the windows.

'Did you not smell it when you got in first?' I said to Dan.

He seemed not to hear me.

'Dan,' I said, 'how could you not smell it when you got in first?'

He waited and then he shrugged his shoulders.

After about a mile Dan pulled over and got out, leaving his door open. I turned and watched him walk slowly away from the truck and stand at the gate of a freshly-ploughed field which rose up away from the road. He stood there with his hands on his hips, head down. After a minute he lifted his head and ran his hand along the top of the iron gate, stroking the rough iron and looking into the field. After a few minutes he turned and looked across the road, down the slope. There was nothing in that field either, only grass studded with clumps of rushes. After a few minutes he came back and got in and drove again.

Mid-Afternoon

I remember that the fields were green and yellow, the green and yellow of tropical birds, and the green and yellow feathers ruffled and turned out in the wind and caught the light and the wind smoothed them out again, smoothing them with a single sweep of its hand like velvet. The waves of light washed over from one field into the next, ignoring ditches and fences. I remember that the ditches of briar and thorn were coming into leaf ahead of the trees, though the ditches always come ahead of the trees. And come summer, the hillsides all around would be gaudy with furze and rape and fields of cabbages lucent blue and striped and scored with ditches of fuschia and buddleia and montebretia, all those exotic refugees from the formal gardens of the local estates and former estates and all the colours would be bright and gaudy and new in the bright light.

It was cool in the cab with the windows down and the wind roaring in the open window and the engine roaring under the bonnet. The wind pushed our hair over our faces and slapped the papers on the floor of the cab and played with our hair, wanting to play. You had to shout to be heard and after a while we were tired of shouting and making our words simple and clear and we didn't shout or talk any more. It was a good excuse not to talk and we were glad to leave the windows down.

In the distance, far to the south, low purple mountains faded into the white haze of the afternoon heat, soaked ink purple, and the blue of the sky fading to white at the horizon. The solid ink was the base of the mountains and the white the paper and all the colours of the ink separating out in-between and bleeding into each other. We still had the windows down. Dan was driving, saying nothing, nobody saying anything anymore, so that it was quiet and loud at the same time. Once I thought I heard a convoy of lorries on some road parallel to our own but I waited and never saw them or their dust. The silence of the countryside, compared to the city, meant we could have heard them well over a mile away, but it was impossible to tell for certain on account of our own engine.

We came to a small village and had to stop to let a flock of sheep cross from one field over the road to another. The gate was at the very corner of the field and on the other side of the ditch, immediately opposite us and right on the road, was a small cottage, a farmhouse, maybe the one that owned the sheep. Somewhere inside someone was playing a cornet. We still had the windows down and we listened, as though we had a choice. The piece being practised was part of a group arrangement and we listened trying to guess what the piece was, the other piece, of which this was only a part. The sheep were soon gone and the road was clear. There was no melody as such and we tried to guess from the rhythm and the cadences. Dan thought it was a religious piece. Jack thought it more military. I didn't know. Jack let on he wanted to go and knock on the door but Dan wouldn't let him. Dan said it didn't matter. He would have been embarrassed even to see Jack go up to the door and ask.

About a mile on there were the skid marks of a truck on the road and a lone trench helmet lying upside down, half-filled with rain. It must have rained there in the night, though the road seemed too dry. But it was inconceivable that the helmet had lain there any longer than that, untouched. Dan tried to clip the helmet with the wheel as we passed and I watched in the mirror as we passed but the helmet lay still on the road in the mirror behind us. The road was not great and the mirror shivered and shuddered against the road ahead and the road behind us shuddered in the mirror but the helmet lay on it still as sculpture, as though the road behind were a landscape painting being held and shaken, with me watching in a mirror to see it being shaken.

'Jack,' I said. 'Please.' He had a big scab on his neck from a fight he'd refused to tell us about, and he couldn't stop picking at it.

'What?' he said. Not to deny it but to make a show of denying it, so that if he stopped picking he'd hear no more about it.

Past Portlaoise every few miles you could see where roadblocks had been. Trenches had been laid and filled in again, the line of earth packed differently and a slightly different colour and pure earth where the surface of the road was all stones. We had come up against three or four blown bridges on the main road and for the time being were driving by a back road. You could see where trees had been felled across the road. These, for the most part had been cut up again and rolled into the ditch, so that all you could see were the lines and mounds of sawdust in the dirt and where it had rained mounds of sodden sawdust and the sections of freshly-sawn trees in the ditch with their new faces of white and yellow wood. A few miles after the helmet we passed sections of freshly-sawn trees in the ditch and their new white faces, the pieces of each tree heaped separately, like an outsized children's puzzle waiting to be rebuilt. A mile on we passed half a dozen bicycles propped up against the ditch, and the trees in the ditch a few yards beyond half sawn through and held upright by old thin ropes draped with branches and the thin lines of new white and yellow three-quarters way into the trunk. When the right truck was on its way they would cut the ropes. The bicycles were there but no sign of their owners. You could tell there was a wall there because of the solid bank of ivy under the briars. Ivy meant a wall. You could see how the sections of wood had been dragged or pushed off the road and the marks on the road and the severed telegraph wires dangling from their posts like broken trapezes.

Nearing Abbeyleix, we came to a roadblock at a crossroads and just beyond the cross was a schoolhouse they'd fortified to command the roadblock and the crossing as a whole. Jack got out and went up to the front and talked for a long time with one of the men in charge, the one who wore a peaked cap.

'When are you going back?' Dan said after a while.

'I haven't decided.'

'Have you not got to be back by any time?'

'I'm supposed to be back Wednesday but I'm not going to be.'

'Why not?'

'Well the funeral won't be till Monday now, so that's Wednesday the earliest we'll be back in Dublin. The earliest. Even if it all goes our way the rest of the way.

'I suppose,' he said.

Up at the front, the man with Jack had taken off his cap and now began to gesticulate grandly. We sat a while more.

'And tell us, Kate, how is she in herself, like?' I said, to be saying something. 'I didn't get much of a chance to talk to her.'

'I wouldn't say she's great now, tell you the truth,' he said.

After a long time Jack came walking back towards us with a lit cigarette in his mouth. I waited until he came up to the door and then rolled down the window:

'How doth the rogue employ you,' I inquired, 'that his bonnet fell with such compliment unto his knee, when you did quit him?'

'It's all sorted,' he said. 'I used to knock a ball against a wall with his brother.'

We drove up past the other cars, saluted by and saluting the men as we passed, and on through the crossroads and past the schoolhouse.

'Well God bless your memory. Sure you haven't played in years,' Dan said.

'It was in his previous incarnation.' I patted Jack's paunch with the flat of my palm. 'Before he came back as a slug.'

The fields looked good when the road rose up over them and they plotted themselves haphazardly into the distance with a harlequin geometry, rising and falling with the hills, plotted with the thick green lines of the ditches that were black in the glare of the sun, and the green and yellow fields white with the glare when you looked at them first, especially those in the distance. It was only those close by or so angled on the hillside as to be spared direct sunlight that revelled in their warm pastel and tropical colours and shook and preened themselves, ruffling and smoothing out their feathers again, demanding admiration.

The rain came soon after the schoolhouse and it came

quickly. I could see it up ahead, on the low hills to the south. The hills to the south were already glittering with rain, the shower advancing steadily up the valley while the sun flourished briefly on the tree-tops and on the ruffled feathers and then fading again and then a wall of water appeared at the far end of the road, approaching implacably, five hundred yards, two hundred, one hundred, fifty, twenty, and then on the roof the distant thunder of hundreds of fists, distant fists, begging entry. It was much darker now. Five hours had passed in two minutes and the ditches and the road and the trees were all steaming and smoking with rain, the rain like veil upon veil of smoke or steam all around us and into the distance, blocking our way, blinding us to all in the distance. But the veils we struck were solid veils, not shredding or ripping but splintering and crackling and scouring over the windshield and the bonnet and the roof. So that we could get used to the notion of solid veils, the onslaught sustained itself with the fortitude and purpose and quiet urgency of a machine. But just as we were getting used to them, the last and lightest of the veils passed over and they moved off into the distance.

In the mirror you could see where it was still raining and where it had yet to rain and where it had rained. The road glistened and the tires hissed on the road and splashed and gulped in the potholes. The whole countryside was glistening and then the sun flourished again and the trees and the grass and the ditches sparkled and the road was bright with light, before and behind, wet light.

Late Afternoon

There was a river up ahead. You could see the sparkle through the trees. There was a small hump-backed bridge with a man fishing from it, one hand held up to his eyes to shield them from the sun and the light on the water.

'We might stop up here and eat,' Dan said. 'Unless anyone has a better suggestion.'

No one had a better suggestion.

He slowed coming up to the bridge. It was a narrow bridge, only wide enough to let one vehicle pass at a time. The fisherman hugged tight to the wall to let us pass. He had his belly to the wall and was looking out over the water and raised his hand in blind salute as we passed behind him. Dan pulled the truck into a gateway just beyond the bridge and we got out and got what we needed from the trunk. The gate was tied shut with an old cracked and buckleless belt and we made shapes that told ourselves we were about to climb over. Behind us the fisherman bellowed and shook his head and jerked his thumb, recommending the field across the road. We crossed the road and went through the gate there and spread our coats on the grass in the shelter of the ditch. The grass was warm from the sun and the ground beneath was cool but dry. There had been no rain here. There was blackthorn in the ditch and Dan had got there first and broken off a piece and he was crushing open and picking at a blossom.

'Ever taste sloe gin? The Vikings were big into it,' he said.

'And look what happened them,' Jack said. He grimaced and shuddered at the very thought. That meant a sloe and his stomach at the same time. Sucking a sloe was like sucking a stone and then you bit into it and made a face. Jack was making the face.

There were three blossom trees in the ditch, one in full bloom, baby pink and all ruffled and crushed like old paper flowers and shedding scraps of pink all across the field in the wind and onto our coats and clothes and into our hair and into the fire when eventually the fire was lit. The other two trees were still clenching their buds in tight and tidy fists of red like berries. Dan undid the newspaper package. There were smaller packages of butcher-paper inside the newspaper and he opened these up one by one:

'Fair ball. She has them scrubbed and everything.'

'A pity we've no rods,' Jack said.

'Sure for what, we've no time,' I said.

'I know. Still, a few hours fishing now would be the business. Another hour or two and that place'll be boiling with trout.' Which meant three hours or four.

He went down to the river-bank, walking along under the row of ash and willow, kicking the grass for wood.

As I went after him, Dan shouted my name after me. I turned and saw him lift his chin an inch and jerk it towards the bridge. With something of a starlet's languor, he brandished an invisible cigarette and lit an invisible match. I nodded that I understood.

I went down, into the shadow of the bridge, where there was a bar of stones wracked with rotten wood. There'd been no rain here for a week and they seemed to have escaped the rain earlier and the river was well down. Falling, it had left behind the wood on the stones. It might swell later with the rain from the land over which we'd come. I'd been surprised to see him fishing from the bridge, but the water was low and the sun, as it stood, cast the shadow of the bridge right onto the water downstream, where the current was quietest, as it so happened. You couldn't cast from the bank for the trees. I collected what wood I could and flung it up onto the bank, flinging it the way you fling wood for a dog. The wood was black and crusted with dead black weeds from the river and after a while my hands were black. There were footholds of a sort up the side of the bridge. I threw up some more wood and climbed up onto the bank beside it and climbed up the footholds as best I could. They were not proper footholds, just gaps scraped out between the stones by those too lazy to go round by the gate and widened and smooth from use. The fisherman was leaning over the centre of the bridge looking into its shadow on the water and shading his eyes.

'Any luck?' I said.

He went on leaning and peering into the water. 'Ara,' he said, 'one or two. I'm only just here. There won't be a rise for a few hours yet.'

'Any size?'

'Pound, pound and a half.'

'It's too bright,' I said.

He had his rod tucked under his armpit lance-like, matches and a pipe and a suede pouch on the wall by his elbow.

'Could we take a few of these for the fire,' I asked, rattling them.

He nodded, not even looking at them.

Just down below, Jack was carrying my wood up to where our coats were. I whistled in admiration and flung the box at him, catching him right in the head. It seemed I hadn't lost my touch.

We talked on and off, looking at the line and at where we thought it ended under the water. I glanced over every now and then to see what progress they were making with the fire, but always my eyes came back to the water. After a while the rod shuddered once and he took a proper grip on it and lifted the tip. The sun glistened on the wet line and beaded the water back into the river and the angle the line made with the surface of the water narrowed as the fish ran towards deeper waters on the far bank, drawing out more and more line from the reel. The further off the line ran the higher the tip rose in the air. The line stretched tight and relaxed and melted into a shallow curve and the sound of the reel changed.

'We might have something here,' he said, winding.

The reel wound with a brittle and metallic strain and the river sucked the little beads of water back down the wet line. The curve became a line again and the angle widened again, almost to ninety degrees. Ninety degrees meant the fish was almost under the bridge. The sound of the reel moved steadily up the scale. There was a sparkle of silver in the shadow of the bridge and he raised the tip of the rod and let it down again, winding furiously as he let it down. The water glittered as it broke and the fish turned and writhed and slapped on the surface of the water as on a hard surface of glass and the fish broke and fell through the glass but leapt straight out again as if from a boiling pan, flashing and slapping and breaking the glass.

'The net there,' he ordered. There was a net with a long handle lying along the narrow grass verge by our feet. Hand over hand, I lowered it towards the water, fifteen feet below, lowering the net away from the rod and when the handle ran out I brought the net closer to the line. The handle was nothing like fifteen feet. There was no breaking glass now. He wound hard and raised the rod in a single smooth action and the fish was in the net. I quickly reversed everything I had done, hand over hand in reverse until I was holding the handle where I'd held it first. I was holding it near the net and the fish was stretching and changing and shaping the net. I let it down onto the ground and the fish bounced on the ground as it had on the glass but now the glass did not break. He stood on the net with a boot on each side of the fish and caught it about the belly with both hands, his hands outside the net, his forefingers and thumbs making a grand circle about its belly. He clubbed the edge of the wall twice with its neck and took the fish out of the net and laid it on top of the wall. It wasn't bouncing any more. The skin was wrinkled now on one side of the neck.

'Good man,' he said.

'She's a nice size,' I said.

'She's not bad, she's not bad at all now.'

The fire was lighting now in the field below, sending up smoke.

'We'll be making tea now,' I said.

He took a few sheets of newspaper out of the oilskin bag at his feet and wrapped the fish in them and laid it in the grass verge in the shadow of the wall. The papers were a week old. It was a Dublin newspaper and I didn't recognise the headlines, though I thought I could guess to what they referred. A little week. He laid the rod and the net along the length of the wall and we walked down to the fire. They asked him about the fish and the size of the fish. He was not overly enthusiastic. He took off his cap and wiped the forearm of his coat across his forehead and flipped his cap on again. Jack had brought up my share of the wood and it was in a heap beside the fire with his own. His wood was white and smooth and rotten and dry and mine was black. Jack was still scrubbing his hands with handfuls of grass, after my wood. My wood cracked and snapped and smoked when he put it on. The wind blustered and the smoke herded us around the fire. Dan poured the tea. There was no milk. We had only two cups and we gave our guest one and used the other between us, drinking fast to pass it on fast and burning our mouths and blowing into the cup before we drank. We poured too much into our mouths each time we drank, using our mouths as cups and swallowing two and three times before our mouths were empty again. Dan had the potatoes boiling but there was nothing else on the fire yet, apart from the tea on the very side. He had to mind and put everything on at the right time so they'd all come ready more or less at once. After a few minutes he undid a little packet and rubbed a scrap of raw fat around the pan, holding the fat with the paper in which it had been wrapped and then throwing the paper into the fire. Once the fat could be heard he took the chops out of their newspaper and laid them in the pan, all hissing and spitting out hot fat, sharp on the skin. For some reason this newspaper had no butcher-paper inside and until it was turned the meat bore the news all mirrored and blurred like an apprentice printer's, the print all gapped and broken and the ink bleeding out of its assigned arenas. Dan turned the chops and herded them round the pan. There were two enamel plates with blue rims the same as the rims of the cups but the fisherman wouldn't take any food. He said that he had to be getting back, that he thought there was a hatch starting, that there would be a rise soon, that the light was just getting right. I could see no change in the light. It was too early and too bright, but he thanked us for the tea and threw the dregs of his tea into the air in a long arc. The arc hit the grass with a flat splash. He set the cup down gently on the grass and reset it a few inches closer to our bundles and tipped his cap and went back up to the gate and up to the bridge and leaned over to look into the water, shading his eyes. There were tea-leaves left clinging to the sides of his cup.

The sausages and the pudding were cooked first and the three of us ate them from the two plates while we waited for the chops and the potatoes to cook. Dan stuck a fork in a chop and cut it where it lay in the pan and lifted it up and studied it and put it back in the pan. We ate the chops and the potatoes with our fingers and with chunks of bread we tore off the loaf, sucking on the bones and pushing the chunks of bread round the plates, leaving swirls on the clean faces of the plates as though they were scoured, swirls that caught the light and made lines of light and eating the bread. We pushed the bread round the plates with quiet intent, not speaking, and then when someone spoke we could not answer except in moans because our mouths were full. When there were only a few streaks left Jack and I duelled on the plate for them with our bread.

'Alright, let's hit the trail,' I said.

When we were finished we kicked at the fire scornfully and used the longer lengths of unused wood to drag it apart and we looked at it shattered and bereft and floundering and dying in fragments on the green grass. The grass was dry but not that dry. Dan threw the dregs of the tea from our cup into the grass in a long arc and rinsed out the tea-leaves that were left clinging to the bottom and the sides of the cups with water, swirling the water in the cups until the water reached the very rim and then throwing the water into the air in long arcs and hearing each arc hit the grass with a flat splash. There was tea left in the pot and water in the pot Jack had brought up from the river and he flung it onto the burning wood in hoarse rages of steam. He could have flung it on the grass but he wanted to hear it rage. We gathered our things and puppetted our coats free of grass and walked back up to the road and put everything back in the trunk. At the bridge he was still leaning and peering. We got in and Dan jabbed at the horn with the heel of his hand and drove off. We were only gone twenty yards when he braked and reversed. He went back past where we'd been parked and stopped and let the engine idle.

'Matches,' he said.

Jack was on the outside anyway. He got out and went over and came back with a lit cigarette in his mouth and something in his closed fist, borne prize-like above his head. At the door he turned his back and did something we couldn't see and weren't meant to see and then got in. He held out his hand, three virgin match-heads jutting out from between the forefinger and thumb, holding them out for us to choose. I withdrew the middle one. A full match, whatever that held in store. But he insisted Dan choose too. Another full match. The third one too, flat on Jack's palm.

'Is that it?' Dan asked him, wary of any expectation in his own voice.

'That's it.'

Early Evening

The best of the brightness was gone out of the day. A few miles on we saw a man on the side of the road up ahead, on foot. As we came closer, he turned and stuck his thumb out.

'Any room at the inn?' Jack said.

'And where are we going to put him? In the glove-box?' Dan said.

'He can sit in the back,' Jack said.

'In the back?' Dan said.

'At least give him the choice,' Jack said. 'No harm asking.'

We slowed and the thumb drooped and dropped and he bent to pick up his bag and we pulled up just beyond him. Jack rolled down the window and he came up.

'How're the men,' he said, looking into the cab. 'Ye're fairly crowded in there.'

'You're more than welcome to hop in the back,' Jack said, tilting his head backwards.

He looked in the back.

'Where you set?' Jack said.

'About five mile down the road,' he said looking down the

road. He looked in the back again. 'Is there bread in the oven?' he said.

'A full loaf,' Jack said. 'There'll be no offence if you let it go.'

He looked in the back again.

'Listen,' he said, 'I'm after riding with hens, hounds, swine and kine. And sure won't it make a *scéal* for the wife.' He swung his bag into the back and went round and climbed in and did a pantomime through the ropes and sat right up against the back of the cab, his bag at the small of his back and his cap pulled over his eyes, mirroring me, his back where my back was and his head the same. Jack had got out and gone round to the driver's door and I had pushed over to where Jack had been, Dan to where I had been and now Jack was driving. I had the window down and the flat of my hand on the outside of the door, the outside of my hand cold from the wind and the palm cool on the cold metal.

'IS IT A HE OR A SHE?' he shouted from the back.

'A HE.' The wind was loud in my ears.

'THAT'S ALRIGHT SO,' he shouted and I heard him settling himself again.

It seemed that the time of the day was where we were on the road. Dublin had been night and Naas dawn. The pub noon, Abbeyleix mid-afternoon. The next town would be evening. Then there would the next one and everything after that would be some shade of night. As though we were driving into the night and could stop and go no further than the evening if we so wished.

The sun was still bright on the white flowers of the thorn trees in the ditches and the furze gaudy with their own brightness and further on patches of water began to appear in the fields again and calves in the rushy fields indifferent to the grass and the breeze grating the surface of the water with light.

'Tell us, do you puck a ball at all over there now?' Dan asked.

'No, never.'

'I thought they'd teams and everything over there.'

'They do. I suppose I just lost interest in it.'

Jack put the flat of his left hand on the dash and raised a finger. Off to our left, the shell of a Buick was sitting in the middle of a field. The bonnet and the boot and all the doors and windows and wheels and seats and inside was gone. But still, a Buick was a Buick. The inside was all hay and hay where the engine had been and a lone dirt-coloured cow eating out of it.

'Jack, I don't mind you doing it I just don't want to see it,' I said. He was picking again. He wanted to say he wasn't but he knew he was and he didn't say anything.

After a while Dan tried another tack:

'And tell us now, the women, how're they treating you over there?'

'Ah now,' I said, 'that'd be telling.'

'For once in your life,' he said, 'could you not just give a straight answer?'

'Looking for tips?' Jack asked.

'I was just wondering,' Dan said, wearily.

'Ah, disinterested quest for knowledge. Very big of you,' Jack said.

Dan didn't answer.

'I never got anything you could call a treat from any woman,' Jack said. 'A treat is what you get at Christmas when you're five years old.'

Dan started to speak: 'So tell us, what ever happened with you—'

'—and they're off,' I said.

'What?' he said, guiltlessly.

'"So tell us,"' I said, '"what ever happened with you and that girl, what was her name?" Is that it?'

'Jesus Christ, I was only asking.'

'Anyway, that's all history,' I said.

'I thought she was your big moment. So what happened?'

'You're asking the wrong man there.'

'I thought ye were getting on great guns.'

'We were, I suppose, for a while.'

'Ah it was longer than just a while now,' Jack said.

'So what was the story?' Dan said. 'Was she not good for it?'

'I'm not even going to say it Dan,' I said.

'Alright alright, I'm only pulling the piss,' Dan said. 'So anyway, what was the story?'

'Your honour?' I appealed.

'Fuck that,' Dan said. 'We're only asking what the story is.'

'The royal plural,' Jack said.

'Listen,' I said, 'it was all very complicated and all very simple. You know the way.'

'Women,' said Dan.

'Dan,' I said, 'don't even.'

After a while there were two blunt thuds above our heads and Jack jumped.

'Christ Almighty,' he muttered, halfway between fright and relief, as he remembered.

I had forgotten he was there too, and it must have showed, because Dan shook his head at the both of us. If he'd been asleep or dozing, who knows how far we'd have taken him.

'Listen, how are we for Durrow?' I asked out the window when we were stopped.

He came round and studied what few scraps you could see of the road up ahead:

'Well, normally ye'd be going grand only they've the bridge down about twenty minutes on, so by rights ye should hang a left just before ye hit that and then a right and that'll bring ye out the far side of town nicely if ye go with it.'

I thanked him and he thanked us and climbed over a ditch into the adjacent field. The ground at the gate was churned up, a grey crust formed on the brown earth from the heat of the afternoon. The falling sun dappled shadows on the mud, as on a choppy lake or a well-tramped beach. In the field a grey cow was standing in the long shadow of the ditch out of the heat of the evening sun. It was hours later before I even thought about the fact that he'd forgone the road for the fields.

About half a mile on we got caught behind a barren hay-cart for a few minutes until it came to a place to pull in and let us pass. We drove on, unsure of our distance from the bridge. It was hard to judge the distance now on account of the hay-cart and we were up to the bridge before we even saw the river. On the road just short of the bridge there was a horse and a man at the very edge of what was left of the bridge pissing down into the water. He must have heard us pull up, but he didn't even turn his head, as if he was deaf. We waited in the cab, not sure who he might be, but the horseman finished pissing and fixed himself and remounted and yanked the horse round and trotted back past us without an acknowledgement of any kind. We waited until he was gone before getting out. Jack looked after him. I went to look at the bridge, though I already knew all I needed to know. The centre arch was gone. You could see sections of curved stone in the water, the water running over them and around them and flattening out again as before. It had been a nice little bridge. It was not much of a river and if the level had been any lower we might have chanced driving down the bank and across. Here too, they seemed to have escaped the rain so far. There was no room to turn, so we backed up along the road for a few hundred yards and turned in a gateway. It was a windy road and we drove slowly, expecting any moment to meet the hay-cart but it never came and we took the turn we'd missed and then the next right as instructed. Very soon we saw the smoke of the town off to the right and then after a time it was behind us.

Evening

Jack: 'Once more into the breach, dear friends.'

'Unto,' I said.

'Into,' Jack said.

There was a long line of vehicles on one side of the road. There did not seem to be any kind of barricade. Later we would see that a narrow trench had been dug three-quarters way across the road and vehicles were allowed pass by laying planks across for one wheel and keeping the other wheel on the verge. But from the back it looked like the cars had simply stopped and queued of their own accord. About the low hills to the south the first sketchings of dusk had begun. At the front there were maybe half-a-dozen soldiers and as many danglers again standing with them, standing around tall and tough. They would stand tall and tough as long as there was no call for them to stand tall and tough. Between cars and carts and traps there must have been a score or more vehicles in the line. People were standing in knots in the evening sun, smoking and smoking pipes and talking, the men in their shirt-sleeves and hatted and bare-headed with their jackets laid across the roofs of the cars as if to dry. Dan looked at his watch and sighed with unintended melodrama. As we sat in the cab an old man passed us pushing a bicycle, struggling to keep going and keep it moving, as though the wheels were stiff or stiff with weight. Hooked over the handlebars was a bag made out of an old pair of trousers, amputated and sewn at the top of the thighs and the waist the mouth and full of empty bottles, the bottles loose in the bag and jostling. It was the fly that gave it away and the jostling gave away what was in the bag. I said I would see what was going on. Jack said he'd come with me. He wanted to stretch his legs, he said. As I was getting out I saw a young woman coming from behind us, one of the occupants of the cars who'd gone for a stroll, I supposed, bored waiting. She was walking along with her eyes on the ground ahead of her. I waited until she was just coming opposite before slamming the door of the truck. Instinctively, she looked over and I caught her eye. That was good enough for me. There were other people around who may have looked over also but I was looking at her and no one else. She just flicked her head up instinctively and looked away again and went on, all at the same pace. That was good enough for me. Jack came over to my side and we strolled up the line at a leisurely pace and very soon we caught up with the old man and passed him out. That was how slow he was going. I had seen him up ahead, but I didn't watch him as we came up to him and passed him out. I didn't want to watch him.

'Have you your smokes on you?' Jack said.

I patted my breast pocket and got out the pack. Some of the cars contained solitary figures, men and women, sitting in silence, reading magazines or smoking. In one car, two old men were playing cards on the green leather seat between them. I put a cigarette between my lips and Jack did likewise and we walked up the line with the unlit cigarettes sticking out of our faces. We'd long since used up the three matches and lit cigarette from cigarette, even when it was only to keep the fire alive, until even that didn't seem worth it. People nodded to us as we passed. The first smokers we saw were a young couple, standing by a big Lancia. She was leaning up against it languidly and he was standing opposite her with his feet apart and looking at her. I could see them up ahead, he with his right arm in a black sling that looked to be a woman's scarf, she relating something to him, making the faces one makes to children when telling them stories, as if recounting the words or emotions of others, simplifying them for the sake of her story, but doing it in a very endearing way. She was absolutely focused on her audience of one. The rest of the world didn't exist. You could almost lip-read her words, so deliberate was her delivery. She had her overcoat draped over her shoulders in the manner of great French generals, the sleeves deflated and hanging limp at her sides.

Jim indicated the man's cigarette: 'Can we take a light off that?'

'Here,' the man said, swiftly transferring his cigarette to his injured hand, pushing it between the fingers, and using his able hand to dig into his pants' pocket. He produced a box of matches and very deftly removed one and struck it on his belt. He'd been practising. Jack cupped a hand about the flame and took a light from it and stood back to let me do likewise.

'*Míle maith agat*,' I said, and drew hard on the cigarette to make sure it stayed lit and held it out from my face to judge my success.

'*Fáilte*,' he said.

'I'm going to go and see what version this crowd have,' Jack said, and he went off up the line.

I looked at the woman's face. She smiled.

'You really did a job on him,' I said, indicating the sling.

She smiled again and she was pretty when she smiled and she was pretty when she didn't. The old man with the bicycle passed us even slower than before, moving very slowly towards the front of the line. I wanted to go on looking at her and I wanted to hear the sound of her voice. I looked up and down the line.

'Nice day for a picnic,' I said.

'It is,' the man said. 'Only we forgot the corkscrew.'

She smiled at that too. It wasn't going to be overly difficult to make her smile. She smiled easy and relaxed. She'd obviously had a lot of practice. They were driving a new Lancia and both dressed very expensively but with taste and discretion.

'Where ye coming from?' I asked.

'Belfast,' he said.

'Get stopped much coming down?' I said.

'Ah no,' he said, 'only every five or six miles.' She smiled at that too.

'We're meant to be on our honeymoon,' she said, smiling. She had a very light American accent. It was soft and well-tailored at the edges, as those of New England are.

'You're not one of the Callaghans of Carlow by any chance are you?' I asked.

There was something in that for both of them.

'On your honeymoon? Without a corkscrew? My condolences,' I said.

'Thanks,' he said earnestly, furrowing his brow and trying to look earnest. 'We appreciate it.'

'We were married in Boston last month,' she said.

'And Mother here said she wanted to see the old country once more before she died,' he said.

'Well there it is,' I said to her, looking around.

'There it is,' she said, smiling.

'Has Mother seen the family plot yet?' I asked.

'She has not,' she said.

Her eyes were slate blue.

'That was going to be a special surprise,' he said.

'Awfully sorry,' I said.

'That's alright,' he said. 'She was going to have to face the music sometime.'

'So what does Mother make of the natives so far?' I asked.

'Oh they seem friendly,' she said, looking towards the front of the line. She made her face a man's face, stern, lantern-jawed. 'On the whole.'

'Oh those are from a different tribe,' I said. 'We don't play with them any more.'

'Mother's very impressed with the standard of English, isn't she?' her husband said.

She clasped her hands together as though in prayer and held them at her throat, breathless with admiration. 'Very,' she said. 'But your French could do with a bit of work. I had a hell of a time ordering wine last night.'

'I'm afraid you'll find our Latin and Greek a bit rusty too. We've had other things on our minds lately,' I said.

They nodded sagely. I could see Jack coming back down the line.

'So where's home?' I said.

'Waterville,' the husband said.

'Going to have a few casts?'

'Father doesn't like water,' she said.

'That makes it an awfully long walk from Boston,' I said. I sniffed. 'What do you for baths?'

'Asses milk,' she said.

'Well, you'll find no shortage of that in Kerry,' I said.

Jack arrived.

'My brother,' I said. 'Allegedly.' I held out my hand to be kissed.

'Mademoiselle,' he said, clicking his heels and bowing and kissing my hand.

'Your grace,' I said, and kissed his hand in turn.

We hadn't used that routine since school. If I had a tie, he was now supposed to lift and kiss the tie, I his braces, and so on, anything we could make use of.

Jack shook hands politely with her and then Father held out his left hand. Jack held out his right, then his left, then allowed himself to get confused and they never actually got round to shaking hands, even after all the antics were over.

His eyes finally settled on the hand in the sling and then on her: 'You did a nice job on him. What happened?'

'Honestly?'

'Well ...' Jack considered, 'just this once.'

'Go on, tell them,' she said. 'He pretends he's embarrassed but he's just dying to tell someone.'

There was a story.

'I was standing on a chair hanging a picture and I sneezed.'

That was the story.

Jack shook his head and grieved. 'No, I'm sorry, you'll have to do better than that. Could you not at least say she pushed you?'

'Waterville,' I said, indicating the husband with a nod.

'Some mighty fishing down there,' Jack said. 'Do you?'

'Her first time,' I said.

'I might,' she said, ignoring me, 'if I had a gentleman to row.'

Jack raised his eyebrows. 'I don't think they let gentlemen into Munster these days.'

'But we're hoping to slip through the lines,' I said. At the front of the line I saw the old man with the bicycle being stopped and his bag checked and then being let through. 'Speaking of which, what news from the front, Captain?'

'The General's on the line to the President. Hold position and await further orders.'

A bunting of green and white was hanging down from one of the telegraph posts to the side of the soldiers and flapping and slapping in the breeze against the side of the pole. At the top it was all twisted and torn and knotted about the wires. In the vacant lane alongside the cars, people were standing about singly and in groups chatting and smoking and two little girls of about five or six were running up and down and weaving in and out of the people with another bunting the same as the first. The two girls were having a lot of fun with the bunting. One of them would take the end and hold it over her head and run as fast as she could with it trailing behind. While we were talking we watched her running up and down as children run, stamping her feet and waddling from side to side, and we watched the starlings massing and spattering the sky and swooping outrageously and unbelievably low and in unbelievable numbers, then suddenly sucked away over a hill and then reappearing again. The other girl would stand at the other end and run after the other end trailing on the ground, stamping and waddling, trying to stand on the end. That was the game. Of course if she stood on it for any more than an instant the bunting would tear and she knew this. She knew she should simply stamp on it once and briefly, as she might have stamped on an insect, but that was too complicated and the bunting began to come away in small lengths each time she stamped. Then they were bored of that game and each one caught an end and they waved it up and down and slapped it on the ground as best they could. The bunting was only about fifteen feet long now but to the little girls that was very long. They ran in and out of the people, one at each end of the bunting. Once the leader had passed one group she would forget about them and not remember that the girl at the rear had to follow in more or less a straight line. But people didn't mind being bumped into and caught up in the bunting. There was no malice in it and they liked to see the girls having fun but the bunting didn't last long like that. It would rip in two whenever there was any real pressure put on it or when it got caught about somebody's legs and the girl at the front kept on running regardless. They really were having a lot of fun and inventing new games to play with the bunting whenever they got bored of the old one.

I looked at the pink sky where the sun was going down and the pinkness of it.

'Well,' I said, 'we'd better go look for that corkscrew.'

'*Au revoir,*' she said.

Jack juggled with phantom hands again and then gave up on it and we all left each other smiling.

I would have liked to take a train journey with her. There can be something very private and personal about taking a train journey together. There are plenty of people with whom I would spend four hours drinking with whom I would not spend four hours on a train.

I walked down the line, hearing Jack's feet behind me, then not hearing them. I stopped and turned. He was ten yards back with his back to me, looking towards the front. I looked to see what he saw. We were still quite close to the front and I could see clearly what was happening there. There were four men in uniform up where the bunting was hanging and clapping and another man in a suit and tie standing slightly apart from them. One of the four threw a punch into the man's stomach and the man seemed actually to lift a few inches off the ground but he stayed on his feet and spread his feet wider and steadied himself. One of the four took the man's belt off and tied his elbows together behind his back and they started to hit him in the ribs and on the head with the butts of their rifles. A van approached from the other direction with its headlights on and the uniforms laid the planks and waved it through and it passed over the planks very slowly and carefully with the driver's head out his window looking at his front wheel. Looking at the front wheel meant not having to look at the man in the suit.

The sky and the hills to the south were grimy and smudged in the fading light. I turned again and walked on down the line. I didn't want to be so close to the front. I stood up against a car and let the van past. On the bonnet of the car was a draughts-board, an interrupted game. One person, at least, had come prepared.

About fifteen yards ahead of our own was a delivery truck with two upright pianos, back to back, covered in oilskins. Going past I raised my arm and through the oilskin tested the lid of the one nearest me. It seemed to be locked and I kept on walking. Up ahead I could see Dan sitting behind the wheel. The way he was sitting in the cab, he couldn't see what was happening up at the front. He was hunched over the wheel and staring at the dash and his lips were moving. He was talking to himself, a few words at a time. As I got closer I could see they were the same few words, repeated over and over, and he was gently nodding his head as he said them and heard what he was saying, agreeing with his own words.

'Looks like we might be a while,' I said loudly and clearly through the windscreen, mouthing my words very clearly and deliberately and immediately tilted my head as if to check the wheels, so as not to be looking at him or let him see me looking at him, so that we could pretend I had not seen him. Out of the corner of my eye, I could see that he had leaned back in his seat and taken his hands off the wheel.

Since I was meant to be checking the wheels, I walked all the way round the truck checking the wheels, came round the front again and leaned up against the passenger door. There was no one near us. After a minute I walked back up to the delivery truck and pulled myself up and lifted up the oilskin and tried the lid again. The one I had tried was locked but the second one was open. There were gaps where some of the chromatics should have been and the ivories were yellowed and dirty like old teeth. I played a C major chord and held it and listened to it and laid an A diminished over it and listened to it fade and merge with the C and listened to the C die to nothing and the A left to fade and die alone. The owner of the truck came back from wherever he'd been and I could tell right away they weren't his pianos.

'Go on, give us a tune,' he said.

I grimaced, as if sorry that I had to disappoint him.

'Go on,' he said, milking his voice.

'Ah,' I said, flapping my hand like a useless hand and closing the lid and getting down, 'I haven't played in years.'

The early evening sky was blackened with thousands upon thousands of starlings, scouring the canvas of the sky with their eccentric swirls and inky strokes and their child-like screams and the rapturous applause of their wings. I walked back to the truck and leaned as before and tried to forget what was going on at the front. I could try all I wanted. Now the man was standing with his legs spread wide, bracing himself against the blows but then they hit him in the back of the head and knocked him right over. His legs scrambled for an instant as he tried to save himself but he fell right onto his face. His arms were behind his back and he had no way of saving himself and he went down right on his face. It seemed as though you could hear the sound of him hitting the ground but of course it was too far away. And even if it had been loud enough it wouldn't have matched up with the sight of him hitting the ground, because of the distance. It was all at a distance and without voices, nothing but the involuntary gasps of the people standing a little further up the line, like little involuntary sighs of pleasure, sighing and gasping like ringside sighs when a good punch is landed and shirking and jerking back their heads as though they were the ones being hit. Immediately he was on the ground he tried to get up again, but every time he got up he was a little less steady on his feet and he took longer to get up. Jack was watching too, a lot closer to the action than I. 'Stay down,' I heard myself ordering him. He had dropped his head onto his chest, maybe hoping to protect it with his shoulders if they started to work on the head. They started to work on the head. One of the officers had gone back up to their tender and come back and was now standing to the side holding a motor-pliers, twirling it in his hands. Or at least it looked like a pliers, from my distance. It might have been better to be closer, up where Jack was, and see what it actually was, whether or not it actually was a pliers, and not to have to be wondering about it. Two of the men had taken off their tunics and rolled up their shirt-sleeves and they had beaten him for a while about the ribs and the kidneys with their fists until their fists were sore. It was not so sore to hit him with the rifle butts. When they were using their fists they had to come in closer and he tried to defend himself with his head. When they came in close he tried to puck them with the head, in the chest and especially in the head. By now he was bleeding a lot. His shirt was all blood and torn to bits and hanging in flaps about him. Eventually, they tore off his shirt and used it to wipe him down and jabbed it at his face to clean the face for their hands, but soon he was all blood again. The soldiers looked at the blood on their hands and on their shirts with disbelief. He, of course, was to blame for the blood. They hit him and he fell and then got up again, taking longer than ever, using the wall at his back for leverage. He went down again and hit his head on the wall as he went down. Some of the people watching turned away with pained faces. Most of the people in the line were watching. Some of the people in the cars had seen the others watching and got out and watched and then some of them got back in again and some of the other people got back into their cars. They sat in their cars with their heads down and their eyes on their newspapers or their magazines. The young couple I couldn't see anywhere. About twenty yards in front of me, one of the little girls was standing in front of her mother, watching. Or a woman I took to be her mother. When the man's head hit the wall the woman took a step closer to her girl and lifted her hand and put it on her shoulder, all the while looking over her head at what was happening at the front. After a while he finally succeeded in getting up again and as he got up one of them caught his head and pushed it down and held it down. They were tired of punching him and breathing heavily. They breathed some more and then two of the men put their rifles across their shoulders and yoked their arms over and started down the line towards us.

Jack saw them come and turned and came down ahead of them. On his way he passed a barefooted girl who had been walking up and down the line, looking for money. She was carrying a tray covered with a cloth that may once have been white. She would stop before a group of people and lift the cloth and negotiate or implore as the occasion demanded until eventually one of them would give her money. Then she would move on to the next group. As he passed her she stood in his way but he side-stepped her deftly and ignored her.

Up at the front, one of the two soldiers remaining held the head down and the other took off his own belt and started to flog him with the thick leather belt on the arms, still tied behind his back. The soft part above the elbows.

Jack came and stood beside me and the two with the rifles

came towards us, holding the rifles by their sides now, one with three stripes on his arm, the other with only one. We stood our ground.

'*Dia dhuit*,' said the three stripes.

We said nothing.

He asked me had I no Irish, asking in Irish. I answered in Irish, saying I had no Irish.

'How long more are we going to be?' I asked him.

He asked me in Irish where I was from. I reminded him in Irish that I had no Irish.

He asked Jack why if I had Irish I wouldn't speak it with him.

Jack looked at me. I looked up the line. The barefooted girl was making her way towards us.

'What did he say?' I asked Jack. I wasn't looking at him or at them, but up the line at the girl.

Jack had even better Irish than me.

'He says the señor has the face of a baboon and why didn't he stay in his tree,' Jack said. Jack said this out loud so that there was no question of the two men not hearing.

'Ask him what he has against the language of Bacon and Dryden and tell him I know well he has it,' I said.

In Irish, Jack said I had no Irish but if he wanted to know something to ask Jack. In Irish, the three stripes answered that he knew I had Irish and he would only talk to me. The barefooted girl came and stood beside us and smiled at us and lifted her cloth. There was some kind of food underneath.

'He says he has a beautiful redhead for a sister and how would you like to make lots of little soldiers with her for the everlasting glory of the nation,' Jack said.

The girl wanted to know if the kind gentlemen wouldn't be pleased to buy some of her lovely gur cake.

'Tell him I already have five wives and my religion permits me no more, but that he should leave a name and address and in the event of the death of one of the five I will most gladly take him up on his generous offer.' I shook my head at the girl.

Jack told him I said he should speak to Jack, that Jack was a wise and honest man, that all decisions in our family were left to Jack and that I was only a fool who had fallen on his head as a child and never been right since.

In English, the three stripes turned to the girl and pushed her away hard and told her he'd already told her to fuck off and he wouldn't tell her again.

'He would know your opinion on the influence of Schopenhauer on Yeats,' Jack said.

The girl came at us again, giving the soldier a wide berth. Once she felt she was within range, she looked at me and smiled and lifted her cloth.

'Does he mean Yeats' early or later work?' I inquired. 'I'll buy the whole lot if you can delineate for me the etymology of *gur*,' I said to the girl. She smiled at me uncertainly.

The polyglot looked at the one stripe, who stared back at him mute and stunned, and then he went round to the side of the truck and looked in the cab and then in the trunk and then in the back, leaving us alone with the one stripe at the head of the truck. Soon he shouted up over the truck, wanting to know what was in the box.

'Guess right and win a prize,' Jack said under his breath.

'Do not stand to him, brother.'

'Not stand? Let those that have sores and noses run,' he declared valiantly. 'Our anger is forging thunderbolts.'

'Thunder?' I scoffed. 'In faith, they are but crackers.'

The one stripe kept looking from us to the three stripes to the girl, not knowing where to look. If anything happened, we wouldn't have to worry too much about him. The girl was still smiling at me doubtfully.

'From the Hindustan, *gur*,' I informed her, 'meaning molasses. You'll know next time.'

The three stripes shouted again, the same words as before.

'O that I had not to tutor myself to speak treason,' Jack said to himself. 'O coward's poor revenge, which dwells but in the tongue!'

We went down to the back and got up onto the truck and undid the ropes. We heard the one stripe shout something else at the girl and she went away. Dan stayed in the cab all the while, saying nothing, not even moving. We stood on the truck with the ropes in our hands. The three stripes got up and looked at the lid and told us to take it off.

We undid the ropes and took off the lid and stood there holding it. They had stolen all of his clothes and he was naked in the box. Jack set his side of the lid gently onto the bed of the truck and I let my side down. He was a good three days old and you could see the new colours coming under the skin. The three stripes seemed not to notice. He held his rifle by the barrel and poked the butt round the inside and then jumped down and started to walk back up to the front with the one stripe. Jack turned and eased himself down and sat at the back edge and tried to breathe, head down. I put the lid back on as best I could on my own. It was more awkward with only one pair of hands. I could see his shoulders rising and falling as he forced himself to breathe steadily and calmly and deeply, imitating a calm person as best he knew how. I waited until the shoulders began to rise and fall more steadily before stepping to the back of the truck and letting myself down. I got into the cab and told Dan. Dan kept staring at the car in front and said nothing.

By the time we were going again the evening was well

drawn in and as they pulled away one by one the cars ahead of us turned on their headlights.

Late Evening

Dan had got out and gone back to Jack. I slid over behind the wheel. When they were ready to go Jack got in and Dan came round to the driver's door and looked in at me and where I was sitting.

'I'll drive,' I remember saying.

'I'm grand.'

'I didn't ask you how you were. I just want to drive a bit.'

He looked at me blankly and walked round the front and got in the other door. I turned the ignition and flicked on the headlights and started to pull out. There were still a few cars ahead of us which for some reason were still being kept waiting. The couple seemed to have been gone for ages, maybe only minutes.

'Mind!' Dan shouted and I jammed on the breaks and there was a cheap thin crack, like a breaking toy. A truck had passed without lights and we watched it move up the line. It moved quickly over the planks and then just as it was rounding the bend up ahead the rear lights came on. It was the truck that had been parked behind us, laden with house-furniture, covered with a tarpaulin, and in the cab of which had sat a bearded man and two Doberman pinschers. All three having remained silent and absolutely still since pulling in behind us, staring out the windscreen and through us all with blank concentration. Maybe they were fed up waiting for us to move.

Jack got out and rubbed his hand along the outside of his door, then hunkered down behind the door and then he sat in again. He set the remains of the wing-mirror on the dash for us to look at if we wanted. I eased out again and drove slowly up to and across the planks.

In the growing dusk we could see the two red tail-lights of the truck up ahead and the tunnel of brightness its headlights made, becoming more and more indistinct the more ground they put between themselves and us. Very occasionally we would meet another car or truck. In the distance their headlights would tunnel a little into the darkness between us and then their lights would be in our eyes and the dusk describing the white lights blackened by the brightness and then the car would pass and the countryside would return with its grey sky. As time passed there was less and less difference between what we saw with the lights in our eyes and what we saw when the lights had passed and then the lights passed and it was still black.

We tried as best we could to talk.

'Well,' Dan said eventually, 'if you ask me, she's an awful eejit to've let you out of her hands.' That was the best he could do.

'That's exactly what I said to her,' I said. 'Those exact words. "Ann," I said, "you don't know what you're letting out of your hands."'

'She never had you in her hands, that was your problem,' Jack said. It wasn't his best, but it was a start.

I ignored him, as I would have done normally. 'I gave her full warning. "Ann," I said, "I'm giving you full warning now. You'll regret this for the rest of your days. Look upon this face, it's the face that launched a thousand ships. Look upon these hands, these eyes. All in the image of God," I reminded her. "What a piece of work is this man," I said. "How noble in reason, how infinite in faculties, in form and moving how express and admirable, in action how like an angel, in apprehension how like a god."'

A car moved up behind us and I adjusted the rear-view mirror so that the lights from behind were not in my eyes.

'She didn't buy it?'

'She didn't buy it.'

'Maybe you need to brush up on your delivery, maybe you didn't say it with quite enough reverence,' Jack said. He was trying.

'Delivery's pretty important alright,' I said.

'Delivery's crucial,' Jack said. 'If you don't have delivery you don't have anything.'

'But words like that should speak for themselves,' I said.

'Should, Madam,' Jack said.

'"Damn it all," I said to her, "if I was a woman I wouldn't have eyes for any other man."'

'Fuck her. She doesn't know what she's missing,' Dan said.

'Well that's just the thing. She does know. She tried it and she didn't like it. If she'd given me the cold shoulder day one it'd be a different matter. A different matter entirely. God knows the hours of comfort I'd've gotten out of that. I could've milked it for all it was worth. But she knows exactly what she's missing, that's the thing.'

'You delighted her not,' Jack said.

'I delighted her not.'

'And tell us now, did she delight you?' Jack asked tenderly.

'She did delight me.'

'That's tough,' Jack said.

'Women,' Dan said.

'Fuck them,' Jack said.

'Fuck them,' I said.

'Fuck them all,' Dan said.

'I'm working on it,' I said.

'You're better off without them,' Dan said.

'You're right,' I said.

'Forget them,' he said.

'I've forgotten them,' I said.

'Better to turn your attention to higher things, to a deeper, more spiritual love, a love as pure as it is perfect,' Jack said, laying a hand gently on my shoulder. He was going more like his old self now. 'It is such a love as there was between David and Jonathan, such as Plato made the very basis of his philosophy, such as you find in the sonnets of Michaelangelo and Shakespeare.'

'And such as you find down Digges Lane of a Friday night.' I shrugged off his hand. I could see him by the lights of the car behind.

'No, do not turn away, do not mock at this love, for it is beautiful, it is fine, it is the noblest form of affection.' He was going full throttle now. I let him run with it. 'There is nothing unnatural about it. It is intellectual, and it repeatedly exists between an elder and a younger man, when the elder has intellect, and the younger man has all the joy, hope and glamour of life before him.'

Dan didn't want to laugh but he couldn't help a little snort at this last bit. The car behind had turned off a side road and he was laughing in the dark.

'The elder has the intellect?' I queried.

At this, I could just see Dan lean forward and lift his fist as if to throw a punch, and drawing away I let myself take the wheel with me, drawing right up onto the verge and racketting along for a few seconds, long enough to let them think about it, before steadying out again.

'No no, all joking aside now, it just wasn't right, the way she treated our boy,' Dan went on. He knew he was meant to react to my driving. 'It was an out and out disgrace.'

'A national disgrace,' Jack said.

'Quite right. Why, I wrote a letter to *The Times* about the thing. An affront to the mores of our society, I said. It was very strong,' I said.

'I read the piece,' Jack said. 'I thought it was awfully tough on the girl. I don't know if I thought it was quite right.'

'Well, if you want my opinion she asked for it, the way she treated our boy,' Dan said.

'I know, but it really was awfully hard on her all the same,' Jack said. 'I hear she's given up her house in the town this season. They say she couldn't bear to face the public.'

'I heard she's gone on a cruise, to Venezuela,' Dan said, trying to lend us a hand.

'An awful business,' said Jack.

'Oh I don't know,' I said. 'I hear Venezuela's pretty nice this time of year.'

We couldn't milk any more out of it.

We drove on, silenced by each other's silence. In the growing dark we could see the two red tail-lights of the truck in the far distance, almost a mile off, I imagined, and just beyond them the tunnel of brightness, becoming more and more indistinct the more ground they put between themselves and us, shrinking, vanishing round a corner and appearing again smaller still.

About two miles on from the roadblock, our lights picked out a figure up ahead, sitting by the side of the road. It was the old man with the bag of bottles, sitting on a milestone. The bicycle was lying on the grass beside him. The grass of the verge was long and poking up through the spokes as though the bicycle had lain there a long time and the grass has grown up through the spokes.

I pulled up and rolled down the window and nodded to him. He was looking off into the distance.

'How's it going,' I said.

He looked at me curiously, as if expected to recognise me.

'We could throw the bike in the back if you wanted,' I said.

'Go on with yerselves,' he said. He looked tired and old and spent.

'It's no trouble,' I said.

He just flapped his hand and stared off into the distance again.

'If I ever get to that stage,' Dan said a minute later, 'I want to be put down.'

I was going to ask for it writing, but Jack got in first:

'And who, pray tell, is going to pay for the silver bullet?'

Up ahead now the two tail-lights sank and surfaced and sank, further off each time, and now there was only one tail-light, sinking and surfacing, further off each time, and eventually surfacing as a mere pinpoint of red and then sinking and surfacing no more.

'You heard about Dan Callaghan,' Dan said.

'I heard nothing.'

'Oh for fuck sake.'

'What?'

'They took him up the mountains.'

I asked them how it happened.

'They pulled him coming out of a bar down off that place, what we used call The Hole In The Wall. You know the place.'

'Was he on his tod?'

'No, but it was only him they took.'

'They knew who they were after,' Jack said.

'Oh they did, no doubt about it. A Sunday morning, coming home for his dinner after a few.'

I said nothing.

'We were all telling him lay low a while and not be sticking his head up out of the trench but sure you know Dan, you couldn't be talking to him.'

'I know.'

'Couldn't ever tell him anything but he had to find it out for himself,' Jack said.

'I know.'

'It was all his own crowd drank in the place and he was well sure of himself. Well sure. Like there was some law against pulling him going or coming.'

'The eejit he was,' Jack said. 'You were talking to yourself, always, talking to that man.'

Had they or anyone any idea who it was?

'Sure what difference does it make?' Dan said.

'No difference maybe. Still, you'd like some name, some trace of them.'

I listened to the engine and listened to the way it strained against the slope now, watching not the road but the top of the wheel, using the sound of the engine to grade the slope and tell my hand when to change the gears. It was a game I always had with myself when I thought I knew the road well enough, only watching out of the very top of my eyes.

'And how's the wife, what's her name, Joan is it?' I heard myself ask.

'Joan. She's not great now. She's gone a bit airy after it, tell you the truth. I don't know, she might pull out of it, it's only two months gone.'

Under the bonnet the engine complained with less urgency now as the road began to level out under us again, the brow of the hill, and from there we could more or less make out what was waiting for us at the bottom of the slope, the lazy arc of a river and the flat and fathomless blackness of it and the slick fast water and the light on the water where it broke or overran itself, the last stale grey light of the day and the brashness of a long queue of headlights on each side of the river, the lights reflected on the glossy blackness along with the eternal orange ember of a fire somewhere that we could not see directly. At the end of the queue on our side were two red tail-lights, perhaps of the truck we'd been following and thought we'd lost.

Late Evening—Night

At the bottom of the hill we joined the end of the queue. In the truck in front of us, a valley had been made in the load to let the driver see behind him. Framed by a set of bamboo dining-chairs, sat the two Dobermans and their owner, as before, still and silent, waiting patiently. Jack said he'd go and see what was going on and we said nothing against it, after his luck with his handball, although it was obvious what was going on. The bridge had been blown and the river was high from recent rain and someone with enough clout himself or who'd got the nod from the local guns had set himself up ferrying people across the river. Everyone had the same simple choice—pay whatever he was asking or traipse who knows how many miles upstream to find a bridge still intact. One thing was sure. The fact that the queue was here now and as long as this meant the next bridge wasn't a mile down the road or five miles.

Whatever heat there had been to the day was long since gone out of it. We stayed in the truck and watched Jack. In the truck ahead of us the head and the heads of the two black dogs remained absolutely still, as before, staring straight out their windscreen as though they knew what they were waiting for and when it would come. We could see them quite clearly through their back window. Dan had warned him against it but Jack went straight up to the truck. I watched Jack say something through the driver's window. The man turned his head to look at Jack and the two dogs did likewise. Jack said something again and pointed very generally at where we'd come from. Nothing happened. Jack laid a hand on the handle of the door and instantly the two dogs bared their teeth. Whether or not they made any sound I could not tell, but Jack took his hand from the door, stood for a few seconds, then turned without looking back at us and strolled up towards the front.

We watched him find the man he wanted and I watched the man and the way he held himself and how he talked and how little he talked and the way he looked at Jack while Jack tried to talk to him.

'His manner doth not please me,' I confided to Dan.

Dan kept looking up ahead towards the river, as if he'd been learning from the dogs.

'Manner fuck,' he said, and then opened the door and rolled and fell out onto his feet.

'Were you born in a barn?' I said.

'The stink of drink off the pair of you,' he said. 'It'd peel paint.'

I looked at him. He put his sole against the panel and slammed the door so hard that I felt it in my teeth.

Jack looked back down towards us over the roofs of the cars and the man looked with him, dutifully, but he was waiting when Jack turned to face him again. Whatever Jack said the man held out his palms, his empty palms, palms with nothing more to offer, and he held the pose and Jack said something and the ferryman wilted a little and then adopted his pose again.

Soon we were watching Jack walking back down towards us. I rolled down my window.

He did not look at the dogs as he passed.

'How much money have we between us?' he said. That was the first thing he said, even before he was up to us.

'How much is he asking?' I said.

'I have, how much have I here?' he said, emptying his left trouser pocket into his right palm and transferring the money into his left and emptying the right. He sifted through the coins, rattling and rearranging and making an estimate and then heaped them onto the bonnet and started to go through his other pockets for paper money.

'What kind of money is he talking about?' I said.

'Look,' he said. 'I'll tell you this much. I'd rather fork out now and cross here and cut our losses, cross here in the light, what light we have left—I'd rather that than drive down God knows how far down God knows what class of road, twenty miles downriver or however far it is and try and find a bridge in God knows what state and try to cross it in the pitch black. For all we know all the bridges are out from here to kingdom come, in either direction. If they've blown it here there's no reason, no reason in the wide earthly world …' And on he went.

He'd got no slack. The boatman had named his price and not listened to a word. He might have named a higher price and let Jack beat him down to what he actually wanted and Jack would have come away that much happier. But Jack had been told take it or leave it. When he'd finished his speech, we looked at him and he let us look.

'It'll be pitch black inside of two hours,' he said.

Dan began to make noises in his pockets.

'How much is he asking?' Dan asked.

Jack said nothing.

'Jesus wept,' I said and got out of the cab and slammed the door.

Jack looked at the car now behind us and at me and at Dan and at the dogs and back at us.

I had a rough idea how much money I had and I set it all on the bonnet, every last farthing, using the coins to keep the paper money from blowing away. Dan did the same, the cheap thin rattle on the bonnet as he set the coins down, cupping his hands the way we had cupped ours, to allow the coins to settle and keep them from rolling off. I looked and judged round about how much it came to. We were still waiting for Jack's answer.

Once our pockets were empty, Dan and I stood in absolute silence and let it grow until in the end he came straight out and told us how much it was per head and how much for the truck. Dan and I let all our air out of us.

'Jesus, Mother of Jesus,' I said.

'That is outrageous,' Dan said, his elocution measured and deliberate.

Now it was Jack's turn to say nothing.

'Sure that's every penny we have nearly,' I said. 'That's nearly every penny we have.'

'That is outrageous,' Dan said.

Jack named the price again and told us that was the price. It was only information now.

'But—' I began, as though I had some principled objection which demanded consideration.

Did we want Jack to repeat himself again? He was perfectly willing to do so.

'There in stone?' I said

'There in stone.'

We had nothing to say, no more than Jack can have had at the head of the queue.

'The juice we've left ...' Jack said, trying to make it easier for us. 'Where are we going on it? What choice have we? We're going to go driving round the country in the black of night and no clue where on earth we are and only dregs in the tank? What choice have we?'

He waited for our answer again and we let him wait.

'We pay the man his money and to hell with him,' Dan said.

'We pay the man his money,' Jack said.

We watched Jack counting out the money on the bonnet, watching not out of distrust but disbelief. He laid the notes down one on top of the other, flipping and switching them round so they were all lined up face up like the bank.

As he laid another one down, Dan said: 'That's the truck and the three of us even there.'

He laid another two down, not looking at us. He gave every one he laid down a name, the amount so far, not looking at Dan, not looking at either of us, as though his entire concentration was required to keep track of the total.

'No,' Dan said.

Dan looked back at the truck and looked from me to Jack.

'No,' he said. 'I don't believe it. I do not believe it.'

Jack held up the wad for general consideration. 'Alright?' he said, looking from me to Dan. 'Alright?' he asked, looking back at me.

He folded the little wad over and put it into his inside pocket and started back for the bank of the river again. I took some coins back from the bonnet and after a while Dan did likewise and we stood around in silence, looking around at the dogs and with our hands in our pockets, not knowing where to look or what to do with our hands.

Up beyond the dogs were some half a dozen farm boys, standing to the side of a long, low cart, rotten and bare. A bottle was being passed around and whatever was in it was clear as water. My eyes had nothing better to do so I let them follow the bottle as it did its rounds, the orbit growing more erratic even in the short few minutes since first I'd spotted it and ever-widening, and I knew that sooner or later someone would hold it out to one of us. Dan saw it too of course. We waited in silence and took our hands out of our pockets and put them back into our pockets and played with the change and the sound of the change and we watched the different lights on the water and what the water did to them and the lights on the far side, where the ferry was loading, a hundred and fifty yards across, give or take a hundred miles. The waters were very fast and strong and muddy with all the rain. Yesterday's rain, probably, all the way down from the mountains. You could see the dirt in the water where it broke or rushed over itself, but the longer we waited the blacker and deeper it became.

Dan turned his back to the river and the drinking.

'Drink and water,' he said under his breath, nodding very generally at the world behind him. 'Two things do not mix. I don't know how many stories I've heard told, about the islanders, rowing it in to the mainland and how many of them are drowned every year doing it. They're out there loading up their boats till they're half under and still on the shore and of course the sea gets up, only they've so much of it inside themselves already they haven't the sense to call off, so of course they drink more of it against their nerves and push off and that's the last is ever seen of them.' There wasn't much could be added to that. 'And they're still at it,' he added. 'Never learn.'

'I don't know,' I said, 'to be that drunk and drown, would it be such a bad way to go?'

'How could you know? Anyone anyway near that drunk is never going to come back for to tell you,' he said, half-turning towards them again, as to an example.

'I suppose,' I said. I thought about it, trying to think what there was in what he said that didn't seem quite right.

'Drinking against the fear and it's the drink kills them,' he said. 'Real Irish sense, that is.'

'I don't know would it be such a bad way to go though, drowning,' I said. 'I don't know would it be the worst.'

'I wouldn't like it,' he said.

'I'm not saying like it. The best is all I'm saying, the best of a bad lot. When you stop struggling, I don't know would it be so bad. A few mouthfuls of water,' I said, and I heard myself saying it. A few mouthfuls of water?

'Even still,' Dan said. 'That moment you know you're going to go. I don't know.'

'You and your moments,' I said. 'I don't think you'd be thinking about drowning at all, not at all. Be too busy trying to keep your head above water.'

The bottle now came to a boy standing only a few feet beyond Dan. If he remained standing where he was, as he was, an offer would be made and he would have to come down on one side or the other. Beyond the bottle, I could see Jack coming back.

'Fire,' Dan said, turning his back to the boys again. 'That must be the worst.' He shuffled his feet, as if resettling his weight, bringing himself a foot closer to me.

'You remember Donney Fleming?' Dan said to Jack as he came towards us again, past the farm boys. Even as he faced us, Jack's eyes went back over his head to the bottle, knowing we were watching him.

'The worst way to go and the best,' I explained.

We remembered Donney in silence. Jack closed his eyes and let his head wander in dismay and disbelief. You couldn't think about him without thinking how he died.

'It doesn't have to be an open boat on a rough sea,' I said, still hearing myself. 'You're as near to it in your own armchair at home, when you think about it.' Fleming had all but burnt to death, falling asleep with his pipe in his mouth, his wife in the kitchen spooning his dinner onto a plate.

'Still, if you thought about it you'd be no more good to yourself. You can't think about that kind of thing.'

'You actually saw him,' Dan said to Jack.

'Sure he only lived over the road, the house on the corner,' Jack said. He paused a moment, cultivating a little expectation. 'I was out on the street knocking a ball up against Clancy's gable. I heard the screams and about turn of course and the next thing out he comes through his front window one big ball of flame, top to toe, hair and all.'

'Out through the front window?' Dan said, as though he was hearing the story for the first time.

'Out through the window,' Jack said. 'You wouldn't think a man had sounds like that inside him.'

'He'd have been better off dying there and then, the state of him after,' I said. I'd said all this before. 'I remember Ma going over to take over from Mrs Fleming, Bridie, for an hour or two when Bridie'd some message to go on. I remember going over with her once, whatever age I was. She had to light his pipe and put it in his mouth for him and hold it for him to have his smoke, he was that bad.'

'He still wanted the pipe?' Dan said, his voice brightening.

'He still wanted the pipe. A hard man, Donney, always, God be good to him. Always the same. He had his ways, and come hell or high water …'

We gave him a moment of silence.

'Anyway,' Jack said, picking the last of the coins from the bonnet, putting his hands into his pocket, 'that's it.' He didn't need to say what he meant.

'I hope he buys a big fucking shotgun with it,' Dan said,

'and I hope his wife comes home blind drunk one night, God forgive me, and sticks it up his arse and pulls the trigger.'

We watched the ferry dream itself across the water towards us, the current rushing and sizzling against its side and rushing round it and the boat more lazy than steady in the water, low and heavy as it was. We looked at the faces of those on board, for some hint of what lay in store for us, imagining ourselves as them but different to them, we having being forewarned by their faces. Even though they themselves, presumably, had watched a boatload of us approach and land at the far bank. They had watched at least once and learned their roles perfectly and now they looked across the water to us, as though we were waiting for them, not for their places.

A man in a torn and cracked oilskin came up behind us and apologised politely for interrupting, so politely that we stopped to listen to him before we had time to think about turning away. When he said he was sorry again I knew he wanted money, but he was shrewd about it, keeping us listening to his story for a while before even mentioning money and even then mentioning it at first only to say that he never asked people for money and he wouldn't dream of asking us now only for the fix he was in, having told us he needed just a shilling more for the fare across, and the story he had to justify his need to cross now, so urgently, something about a sick daughter, if the gentlemen would have just a little to spare between the three of them, and telling us how much difference it would make. Of course we had all heard these stories before and never knew whether or not to believe them, but we wanted to believe him, we wanted to believe his story if only to allow us to give him money without feeling we'd been fooled, so that he could stop asking us for money, to relieve him of the shame implied in his assertion that he never begged for money. We hadn't much left after what we'd given to the ferryman, but the oilskin wasn't asking for much, and the claim that so little could make such a difference, and maybe the fact that ferry was just about to leave, the last few stragglers getting on, and we—as arranged—only waiting until all but the space for us was filled, and the sense of quiet urgency this somehow added to his predicament—all this or something else entirely made Dan put his hand in his pocket. I put my right hand on Dan's arm and took my left out and counted into the waiting palm some of the coins I had, eventually making up a shilling. Jack was in the cab running the engine and waiting for the word. Dan and I were to walk on, less weight in the truck.

After mooring, gangplanks had clapped and slapped on the bank made muddy by previous traffic and when the deck was empty without any signal those in the line had begun to move forward to take their places. I had watched the side of the ferry emptying and watched more and more of it appear above the water, plank by plank, until it was absolutely empty and the first of the cars drove on.

Now, the oilskin looked dumbly at the coins in his palm and looked at me with the same expression, the same blank distress in his face as he'd first presented to us, as though approaching us again for the first time.

'Just half a crown,' he said.

I looked at his face, wanting to see another face there.

'A shilling you needed you said.'

'Just half a crown,' he said, in disbelief at our miserliness.

'You said you needed a shilling, we gave you a shilling,' I said. If we could just restrict ourselves to the exchange of information.

He turned without a word and walked on to the group of men standing behind us, who would have to wait for the next crossing, and started up precisely the same spiel, with precisely the same tone and gestures as before, like a reliable rep actor.

The boatman stood up on the ditch watching indifferently the progress of his passengers. Dan and I walked alongside the truck as Jack inched it forward. Dan gave his grunted greeting a nod but I passed him by without looking at him or acknowledging him. Jack stopped a few yards short, waving the last of the foot-passengers on ahead. First aboard, now parked at the prow, was the truck ahead of us, the dogs, being the biggest and heaviest load after ours, to balance which Jack had been instructed to wait until last.

'Come on,' Dan said to me.

With the farm boys it was all horseplay at the water's edge, one pretending he was about to push another in, feinting and bobbing like featherweights, and everyone watching and laughing and trying to suppress their laughter. Whatever happened was waiting to happen, what with the mud and the dying light and all the space now in the bottle. The next time I saw them, one of them would be wearing an appalled, grief-stricken face, a foot above the shallow water by the bank, his body stiffened in the pose in which he'd landed, on his backside, arms behind him for support. He would be shocked at his shock, how forgetful it was of all the daring there had been in their play. His friends would be standing around laughing, albeit silently, out of respect, and shaking with silent laughter. But that would all be half a minute later, when I was boarding the ferry.

The ferryman was on board and shouted to Jack and waved him forward.

'Come on,' said Dan's voice behind me. 'To hell with him.' Somewhere to my rear, between me and the ferry, I could hear a woman talking deliberately in Irish to a child. I had seen them a little earlier. The boy had a toy bow and arrow. I had my eyes on the oilskin but I was trying to follow the woman's words. I could only follow the barest gist of what she was saying but it was obvious that the child had reservations about getting onto the boat and she was making up stories as to why she had to give money to the nice man with the boat.

I looked over my shoulder at the ferry and Jack wrestling with the wheel and the truck slowly wriggling into place and the ferryman watching him too, waiting to raise the side, and looked back again at the oilskin with his hand held out to the men who'd been behind us to show how many coins he already had and how few he needed. I took five or six good strides and I was up to him, coming at him from the side so he couldn't see me coming. All he could see was the changing expressions in his audience and at the last second he looked around to see what they saw but by then I was on him and had him by the ear. I held the ear three or four inches higher than it would normally be. He looked me in the face to see what I meant by this and held out his hand, holding out the money at me and tried to look at it again himself, as though there'd been some mistake in his calculations. Some of the men facing him may have said something. I had him teetering on his toes and had one leg out behind and led him back over it and let him buckle backwards into the mud. I stepped over him and picked up three coins out of the mud and looked at them in my palm to see what they were and turned and strode back to the ferry, where Jack and Dan were waiting for me. I stepped on, ignoring the ferryman and whatever it was he said.

The farm-boy who had ended up in the water was now standing in the water, his dripping arms out from his sides, as though they were the only wet part of him. His friends, already aboard, held out hands to pull him in over the side, but he waddled round to the gang-plank ineptly, learning to walk again and making the ferryman wait. Once aboard the wet boy stood on his own, a little apart from his friends, his wet clothes weighing him down and reshaping him. The sight of him and how wet and cold and miserable he was and his new mood had blunted completely the playfulness they'd all had at the water's edge.

As we moved out from the bank I looked back, hoping to see something new in the beggar's eyes, or at least to see him watching us as we moved out. I saw that all three of us were looking back towards the shore, but he was too concerned with another group to even think about the ferry or the river. To him all they were, all we were, was a queue and the common cause in the queue and the chance of playing on it.

The ferry moved fairly flatly and sluggishly across the current. Ahead of us the cable stretched taut and hard and straight over the water, drawn through a contraption driven by a tractor-engine, or what looked like a tractor-engine to me. Behind us the cable hung limp and dragged in the water. The sound of the engine filled the air and the night but it was nothing to the sound of the water moving around us and rushing against the side. Going by its sound, the motor should have been sufficient, but a few feet ahead of the engine the ferryman leaned forward and gripped the incoming cable with both hands and let himself fall backwards, using his falling weight for strength, not pulling as such, then pulled himself upright and leaned forward and started again. If he'd pulled he would have been worn out long ago. I watched him leaning and falling a while, and the rhythm of his rise and fall, and let it work on me.

For reasons of space and weight, the truck with the two Dobermans had been put as far forwards as possible. I had gone and stood beside it because I wanted to watch the way the ferryman was working in the very prow and because I didn't want to see the oilskin anymore. The dogs were alone in the cab, their ears pricked and their heads still and their tongues loose and dripping, looking out across the water to the other shore and the lights there and the figures moving in and out of the lights. I couldn't see where their owner was. Looking at the arrangement of vehicles on the ferry, I didn't understand the arrangement of weight and space, but presumed he had some system. Certainly he'd taken a lot of time and trouble over boarding us.

The boat rolled a little as it moved across the water, though less like the rolling of a boat in the sea than a slow, lumbering parody of the motion of our truck on the road, the passengers' heads all rolling and righting in a perfect choreography with each buffet of the current, and not only the heads but the lamps hanging from the carts and the stirrups of the horses and the bell round the cow's neck and the heads of the two Dobermans.

The woman and boy were beside me, right at the prow, to the side of the ferryman. The woman was still trying to talk to the boy, but the boy was no longer talking, no longer even listening to his mother. He had his arrow on a string and was firing it ahead of the boat, up into the air and out into the current ahead of us and watching the current whip it away and then drawing it back in over the side. His mother went on trying to talk to him, and I watched her transferring her ring from one finger to the next as she spoke and tried to get him to speak. I remembered the feather I'd seen in the straw of the cart with the hens and went and got it and stuck it in his hair, a black raven's feather. He was unimpressed. I tried to talk to him, but their dialect was unfamiliar and I knew I could only say very basic things and ended up saying only what I was able to say, rather than what I wanted to say, though even that was hard to imagine in that particular dialect, as I couldn't imagine the way they might say it or if they would say that at all. I tried to stop myself before I felt completely useless but felt useless anyway. The boy had decided to sulk and wouldn't let himself even register my presence.

Most of the rest of the passengers remained silent, avoiding each other's eyes, as if ashamed to be in the other's presence, or ashamed to put the others in the presence of someone reduced to paying such an outrageous price.

We were nearing the shore. I looked at my brothers and saw they were talking and went back to them. Dan had his back to me. Jack smiled over Dan's shoulder as he saw me come and put his hand on the shoulder:

'You may die young,' he consoled Dan, turning him to face me, 'but at least you'll make a good-looking corpse.' I had no idea what they were talking about and didn't ask.

Whatever little bit of light had remained when we'd first joined the queue was gone by the time we touched the other shore. With the twilight still tempering the headlights a little, from the queue it had seemed just possible to make out the shapes and figures on the other side, waiting for us, but by the time we got anywhere near them the last of the natural light was gone and they were just black blurs melting in and out of their own headlights.

From the bank of the river, the road we wanted sloped upwards again, steeply, and the engine struggled with the slope and I struggled to change the gears without coming to a halt. Dan and Jack remained silent, staring ahead. Eventually, under the bonnet the engine began to complain with a little less urgency. As we mounted the hill, our lights rose off the ground and I stopped, the better to see, our lights pushing ahead a little distance at a level with us. Down below, we saw on the road ahead yet another line of lights, red and white. The cars and carts could be made out by the headlights, those left burning, and by the light of a large fire on each side of the road at the head of the line, making silhouettes of the men immediately in front of them.

Night

I eased off the hand-brake. At first the truck seemed not to move. Jack began to bounce up and down in his seat and I did likewise. Dan would not join in. We could feel her moving, the wheels stiff and sluggish and sleepy at first, then gathering a little momentum, and then the tires' torrent in the quiet night and the truck careering along. We were travelling at no extraordinary speed, yet it felt much more reckless than if we'd had the engine and the lights on. The line of cars began on the far side of the trough in the road and I wanted to try to reach them without the engine so I kept my foot off the brake. We were really travelling now and we weren't even to the bottom of the hill yet.

'Jim,' Dan said sternly.

Jack laughed and threw back his head and clattered his palms on his thighs and let out a feral howl, bringing it up from deep inside him.

She eased into the flat of the trough and then up into the gentle slope without seeming to lose any pace and then cruised a while and then the sound of the tires began to die a little. It was a good stretch of road. I actually had to touch the brakes ten yards out, very delicately, just letting myself know I was in control again, and then I let her roll all the way, letting her go as close as possible to the bumper of the car in front.

'You just touched her,' Jack said.

'My bollicks.'

'Pound to a pinch of shit.'

'Sold! to the gentleman in the twilled-silk wedding-gown!'

He rubbed his hands greedily and jumped out and swaggered up to the front and his features melted. He pulled his hair and stamped up and down. I got out and went to look, fighting hard not to smile. There was hardly an inch between the bumpers. I rubbed my forefinger and thumb together and blew him a kiss.

He threw back his head and raised his eyes to heaven.

'Why? Why?' he cried, forlorn.

Dan stuck his head out the window and told Jack to quit acting the maggot and walk up front to see what the story was.

The night was growing cool and I got back in the cab. Most of the men at the head of the line seemed to be other drivers, some from the ferry, although there was no sign of the one with the dogs. He must have turned off somewhere, or somehow been let through immediately. From where I was I could see only one soldier. Although it was quite a distance, you could tell he was a soldier because you could tell he was wearing a waist-belt outside his jacket, its S-hook buckle shining in the headlights. The headlights of the first car were not on and the other headlights did not shine directly on the men at the front. With the light from the fires at their backs, the men were no more than flat fathomless cut-outs till they moved into the headlights, but even so the silver S stood out against the dark

Cormac James

cloth of the soldier's tunic, moving back and forth across the road.

'We were all glad you could come home Jim,' Dan said.

'What else was I going to do?' I said. 'I was only sorry I didn't get back in time. I never thought he was so bad.'

'Sure there was none of us any of us thought it. You never think it till you're sure and when you're sure it's too late.'

'I know.'

'I never thought it either,' Dan said, 'till near the end.'

'Was he very bad?'

'Ah, he was bad enough in the finish.'

'Jack said he was very bad for a while.'

'He was bad alright coming up to the end,' Dan said. He was staring straight ahead. His left hand lay on his thigh. His right hand lay flat on the seat between us, his thumb rubbing back and forth across a ripped piece of the leather.

'How did he take it?'

'I don't know, he took it alright for a while I suppose, but it was fairly hard on him coming up to the end. The doctor was telling him he was grand but he knew well. And he started remembering then. All about when we were lads and all that.'

'He knew he was fucked.'

'He did, I suppose.'

Up at the front, as far as I could make out, the fires consisted of heaps of wood and some kind of sacking or rags. The colour and the filth of the flames said paraffin too. Rags soaked in paraffin, maybe. The flames flared up and swept down over the ground in the wind and the smoke was black and dirty in the white light of the headlights. I could recognise Jack's cut-out from behind, flat and deep. Facing him was the cut-out with the shining S in the centre. Jack came strolling down the line, the S alongside him. They came closer and I could make out the

127

soldier more clearly. He seemed to be unarmed and he walked like a farmer. He was very big and broad and there didn't look to be much give in him. Jack was chatting away and the farmer was saying nothing. You could see them moving in and out of the headlights, their shadows stretching out to meet us at first from the light of the fires and then giant and eccentric back beyond them as they moved into the headlights, the shadows parodying their approach with a lanky strut. Dan and I were still sitting in the truck. I rolled down the driver's window as they came up and held out my hand. He may not have much wanted to, but he held out his hand. I gripped it hard and shook it hard and held onto it. There was a strong dirty smell of burnt paraffin in the air.

'Be more near to us,' I said. 'Welcome, nearer yet.'

Unseen, Jack doffed his cap and made legs to our distinguished guest.

'Let's have a look at this thing,' he said in a thick accent, drawing away his hand.

'Some believe brusqueness becomes the air of a man well, thinking it argues service, resolution and manhood,' Jack conceded. 'But let not—'

'Get out or ye'll be sorry,' he said, curt and low.

'Oh take me not in haste!' I pleaded, getting out. 'I have great sins, and must have days, nay months, with penitential heaves, to lift 'em out, not to die unclear. O, thou wilt kill me both in heaven and here!'

'You too boyo,' he grunted in at Dan.

Dan got out.

The air smelled of burnt paraffin and nothing else and the horses did not like it. There was a pair of horses in front of the car in front of us and more up the line. The smell of paraffin made the horses uneasy and they stamped and snorted and flared their nostrils and shook themselves restlessly and tested their tackle. Further up again a man patted his horses' necks and spoke to them quietly and discreetly, taking them into his confidence.

We went to the back of the truck and looked up into it.

'This man and his words appear to me great strangers,' Jack confided in me.

'Time and our swords may make him more acquainted.'

'Go on,' he grunted.

Jack got up onto the bed of the truck and started to undo the ropes. Dan started undoing some of the ropes on his side. The ropes went over the wooden slats of the side and were tied on the outside. Two would be as quick as three. I would only have got in their way. I stood and watched the crows all along the ditch watching us curiously. About a hundred yards back the road, a herd of cattle of about thirty or forty head were slowly making their way towards us, apparently of their own accord. I could see no one driving them. It was difficult to make them out in the darkness. In the darkness the cattle were just a moving mass and the sound of their hooves, gradually growing louder and louder. When the ropes were untied, Jack turned for further instructions.

'Go on.'

'Give us a hand here,' he said to Dan.

Dan climbed up and they took off the lid and carefully laid it against the side. Jack's coat and my coat were laid over him. The farmer climbed up and looked in.

'Right, empty it,' he said.

Jack and Dan looked at him. I looked at him and looked at Jack and at Dan.

'Jack,' I said.

'I won't say it twice,' he said.

'Jack,' I said.

The first of the cattle were up to us now. The hooves were loud and growing louder all the time.

'Empty it,' the farmer said to Jack. He had his back to me all the time.

'Jack,' I said.

'Listen you boy—' he said, turning to face me.

Dan jumped down off the bed of the truck, hitting the ground with a short, sick moan, and stood with his back to the farmer, looking at the cattle. The cattle were all around us now. The cattle were all black and black in the night and their hooves were heavy and loud on the ground and the sound of their flanks thudding against each other was dull and flat and strange. Jack backed up and leaned against the back of the cab and folded his arms. The farmer turned to Jack and took a step towards him. He was much bigger than Jack and he knew it. Jack had his arms folded and was leaning backwards very casually against the back of the cab, as though listening to whatever the farmer was saying. As the farmer stepped towards him, Jack stood up straight again with his palms offered in surrender—he didn't want any trouble—and his right leg swung up very fast and caught the farmer right in the bollocks with the toe of his boot and the farmer folded in two like a rag-doll and Jack seemed to continue the momentum of his leg, bringing the knee right up into the face as the face came down to meet it. Of course, there could be no force to speak of in bringing the knee up, it was meeting the head coming down that made it work, the head coming down as the rag-doll folded in two. It was very smooth and well done and perfectly timed and very nice to watch. You could hear the crack as the knee hit the nose. The farmer stumbled backwards with his hands still at his side and his tall broad frame crumpled at the knees and the waist. You could see that on the second step backwards he would trip over the coffin and on the second step his legs hit the side of the coffin and his legs went right out from under him and he fell onto his arse like a man on ice. Jack took a stride with his left leg and swung his right leg at the head in a long graceful arc as if taking a free-kick off the half-way line. The head flapped back and bounced off the side of the coffin and fell limply onto the bed of the truck. It was only now, when it was too late, that a hand came up to hide the face and instantly, as though squeezing a sponge, a lot of blood started coming through the fingers, the blood black in the darkness. At the same time the other hand reached out to catch Jack's leg and Jack hopped backwards and over the side of the truck and onto the ground with great agility. It was all perfectly choreographed and executed and very impressive to watch. I took a step forward and grabbed the hair with both hands. I knew he was heavy but he didn't feel heavy and I had no trouble pulling him off the truck. When he was about half-way off he realised what was happening and what was about to happen and started to scramble with his legs but it was too late. He hit the ground like a bag of sand, with the same blunt hiss. One of the eyes was clenched shut and the other one was all blood. Jack stepped over and started kicking him in the stomach and talking to him through his teeth. He was jeering him to get up and kicking him in the stomach. This was all in a few seconds. The cattle were still around us.

'Keep an eye out,' I ordered Dan. That would let him go up to the front of the truck and I knew he'd be glad to do it. We were still the last in line and it was dark at the back of the truck, with only a very dull glow from our headlights and the headlights further up the line. The blood on his face was black and slick in the dull light and all down the front of his tunic was black and slick and the S much harder to make out.

'Will I knock the lights off?' Dan asked, with something very young in his voice. It was even stranger, even younger, because he had to speak loudly, over the hooves.

'Do no such thing,' I said They wouldn't be able to see through them.

He went up to the front of the truck. The hooves were loud on the road and all around us and we could hear them up the line now and back in the darkness, the hooves of the cattle yet to come.

Jack and I both were breathing loudly, standing over him and looking down. He was coughing hard and then he rolled onto his side and puked hard. I had to jump back to mind it didn't get on my boots. A cow would come upon us all of a sudden and turn away in a kind of awkward modesty, bullying into the others to avoid so much as touching us.

'Let him up,' I said.

When he was finished puking he rolled over and drew up onto his knees with his face in the dirt and his backside in the air and pushed himself up and swayed on his knees.

'That'll do nicely,' I said.

I went behind him and caught him tight by the hair to hold him up and started punching him in the side of the face. I was hitting him in such a way as not to destroy my wrist, keeping it stiff and hitting him straight so that the shock went straight up the arm, hitting him from the shoulder. I'd been playing tennis all last year and just started again, and my wrist was fairly strong. I was hitting him in the face. I was talking to him through my teeth. After every few words I hit him again. I turned his head to hit another part of his face. I flexed my hand and clenched it tight again and hit him again. He was all bloody and cut and puffed up and both eyes were shut now and he didn't have much of a face any more. I kept hitting him where his face had been. What was his face? Only something his mother and father had given him. Nothing to do with him. I'd give him a new face. I was hitting him slowly and deliberately where his face had been. His face was something they looked through to see the faces of his mother and father. I'd give him a face they'd look through to see the face he had before.

He let out a little grunt every time I hit him but other than that he didn't seem to register the punches much at all now. And his weight was starting to tell on my left hand, holding him up for my right. The grunts were not altogether unlike the grunts of the cows. Far off, at the head of the line, the sound of the hooves was like running water. Like running water. I hadn't noticed that before. I kept hitting him but the punches seemed to have little effect and eventually my hand got so sore that I let go of his hair and he crumpled onto the ground like a rag-doll. They always say it's like a rag-doll but it rarely is.

A cow stalled and cocked its tail and dribbled shit onto the ground by his head.

Jack nudged him in the side with the toe of his boot.

'On your feet soldier,' he ordered.

He lay there not moving, like something that was not meant to move.

'Centuries of oppression have almost extinguished the military spirit of Ireland,' Jack said, shaking his head in disappointment. 'And once gone, it will be very hard, perhaps impossible, ever to arouse her again.'

Dan came down and looked at him and how he lay. 'Sweet Jesus,' he said. He looked at me and listened to the sound of me.

All this time, I seemed to have forgotten to breathe, and now I was trying to breathe again, both for myself now and for the one who'd forgotten to breathe.

'I can't see anyone else up front,' Dan said.

The farmer was just a heap on the road, like a heap of old clothes.

'Help me here one of ye,' Jack said. 'And get a move on.'

The last few stragglers of the herd were going by.

'What are you going to do?' That was Dan's voice.

'Watch and you'll see.' That was Jack.

'Was there no one else up there?' Me, to Jack.

'If there was I didn't see them.'

'What'll we do with him?' That was Dan.

'We will teach him to be pure, truthful, honest, sober, kindly; clean in heart as well as in body,' Jack said, catching the farmer under the armpits.

I caught the heels and we waddled towards the ditch.

'We will teach him to be generous in his service to his parents and companions now, as we would have him generous in his service to his country hereafter.' Jack's voice was tight with the weight of the farmer.

We waddled up onto the top of the ditch and swung him back and forth, building up height like a swing and finally we let him fly. There was a splash from inside the ditch but it was too dark to see anything. Dan came running up bent low and ploughed into us both, toppling us over into the field.

Dan and Jack had instantly pressed themselves to the inside of the ditch but I was too slow, and now I didn't want to move in case whoever it was saw me moving. Like them, instantly I had dropped to my hunkers and he might not see me but he might see me moving. Or that I was no longer where I had been. Outside the ditch the footsteps went by in the dirt. Maybe it was he who'd been driving the cattle. Dutifully, the feet chewed their way along the dirt. The feet went by and then stopped. I didn't even dare turn my head to see where they were, but I knew they had not gone very far past. My ears were full of sounds I couldn't stop myself making. I was trying not to breathe and to breathe quietly.

'Who's there?' the feet said, low and meek.

I said nothing. I didn't even dare turn my head. I didn't know if he had a gun or if there were another half-dozen like him two hundred yards down the road or if he was the one who'd been driving the cattle.

'Is there somebody there?' he said, louder.

'Jesus Christ,' I snapped at him, 'can't a man even take a shite in peace in this goddamned country now?'

He mumbled something. Maybe it was just a mumble of surprise. The feet went on down the gravel. Once the feet were gone all I could hear were my heart and my breathing.

'I thought you said there was only the one of them,' I hissed at the dark.

'There was. Maybe it's only another driver.'

'Maybe. We want to get the fuck out of here, and pronto.'

We climbed back up over the ditch as quietly as we could, but on the top of the ditch I stopped and told them I'd be with them when they were ready, as though I really did need to hunker down inside the ditch. While they fixed the lid and the ropes again I went back inside the ditch and stripped him, quickly. It was pitch black there and I had to work by touch. I was afraid he might have shit himself, but at first, taking the trousers off, it seemed he hadn't. He had good thick underwear and long shirt-tails and it hadn't soaked through.

'Jim,' Jack said, when he saw the uniform. 'If we get caught with that in the truck.'

'What do you want it for?' Dan said.

I put the bundle under the folded tarp beside the trunk. If we saw we were going to be stopped again, I would ditch it.

'How do we look?' I said.

'Give your hands a quick wipe in the grass there,' Dan said. My hands were all slick and black. 'And take off your jackets the pair of you. And here.' He licked his forefinger and wiped a spot on my cheek. It was the same finger our mother used. 'Ye're grand now. You sit in the middle,' he said to me.

Dan was driving. He let off the hand-brake and we rolled back a few yards and he put the hand-brake on again. He fired the ignition and shifted into gear and pulled out past the line of cars and drove on up the wrong side of the road. They were all turning their heads and looking at us. None of us turned our heads but we were watching out of the sides of our eyes.

'How're we fixed?' Dan said.

'I can't see a sinner. Take her easy but keep going,' I said to Dan.

The cart they were using as a barricade stood right in the middle of the road and Dan had no trouble swinging the truck around it, up onto the grass and onto the road again. The wheels just caught the edge of one of the fires and dragged it apart and left a ragged line of fire along the road behind us. After a hundred yards I leaned towards Dan and looked in the rear-view mirror and saw the trail of burning rags and the white lights beyond them shining into my eyes. No one in the line of cars seemed to be making any move but it was almost impossible to tell with the lights in my eyes. I wondered how long they would wait.

I was holding the wrist of my right hand, supporting it. 'My hand is fucked from that bogman's thick fucking skull,' I said, and placed the hand on my thigh and let it rest there.

Dan leaned against me gently, to lean back to where I'd been so he could glance in the mirror himself, narrowing his eyes against the lights.

'You should have used your own head,' Jack said. 'He'd've never again got up.'

Night

I remember that Jack had hit his nose on his knee jumping over
the ditch and now his face was all blood. He'd looked for
something to soak it up and we'd found some old handbills in
the glove-box. They didn't seem much use at soaking much less
stanching it, but for want of anything else he had them up to his
nose and his head back and kept dropping his head to check if
the bleeding had stopped and why it wouldn't stop, until
eventually it stopped. That left a lot of blood on his face and in
his hair. I had blood on my shirt and on my hands. I had wiped
my hands clean but they were all blood again.

'We can't get stopped looking like this,' I said. 'We're going
to have to clean up someplace. Keep an eye out for a pump.'

We drove a while and there was no pump. Up ahead there
were dim lights in the tall windows of a church at the side of the
road and as we came closer we could hear a choir singing,
weakly, but we didn't slow down. All I gathered as we passed
were a few random notes and they were unfamiliar and seemed
unrelated. Once we passed the church we could see a fire by the
roadside about a mile up ahead. It seemed quite distant in the

night and we could see no headlights, but it was definitely by the side of the road or on the road. Dan pulled up and began to reverse. We had passed a small farmhouse just beyond the church and he reversed as far as that. He got out, slamming the door, and went and knocked on the door. The door was right on the road. He knocked again and after a minute a young woman opened the door a little, showing a long thin strip of herself in the gap between door and jamb.

He said something to her, something about needing water for the radiator he said later, but she craned her head and said something back to him, opening the door more and craning her head to look around him. He had stood himself between her and the truck but she stepped around him and took a few steps closer to us, the better to see who we were. Jack swung open the door and stood out, unafraid of being seen, now that she'd seen us. She turned around to Dan again.

'We just need a drop of water to clean up. We'll be gone in five minutes,' he said. 'Please.'

She looked at us again and looked up and down the road. The road was dark. She looked back inside into her dark hall and looked back at Dan.

'There's a pump in the yard out the back. But ye'll have to be quick.'

Dan nodded at her that he understood and nodded for us to come round the back. She pulled out the front door behind her and went round the side of the house with Dan, Dan nodding for us to follow them around. Jack went ahead but I paused a moment to listen to the choir. They were singing in Latin. I preferred when it was Latin. My Latin was rusty and I liked it that way, because I could only guess at what the words meant. For all my guessing, I could tell that for plenty of those singing the words were only sounds. They didn't pronounce them as they should have and the voices only toyed with their sounds and the number of voices blurred the sounds and the shapes of the words, one soaking into the next. That suited me fine. I only wanted to hear them lift up their voices. The voices were dutiful and conscientious but not particularly enthusiastic. But then the hymn began to move towards its conclusion with some air of inevitability and despite themselves the voices were being carried along by the momentum and then one voice lifted itself above them all, a woman's voice, strong and determined and calm and demanding attention. I was glad I didn't know the exact meaning of the words, so I could doubt or dismiss all I could have guessed at. I didn't want to know what the words meant, what they might not mean. The words were empty shapes and the singers were breathing life into them. The words were just shapes, balloons, waiting to be filled, and the voices filled them with warm air and they hung in the air because they were warmer and then the air cooled and leaked away and they were shapeless again.

It was an old cobbled yard enclosed by a cowshed and a few outhouses, all much older than the house itself. The pump was to one side and Dan was working it. It was well oiled and worked quietly. She was standing a few steps away, watching Dan work the pump. There was a young fair-haired boy of about six or seven in the yard watching us. He had the windpipe of a goose in his hands and was blowing into it whistle-like and making a sound like a goose. It was impossible to say whether the windpipe or he himself was the goose. The boy blew and the goose screeched. We could see it all by the light from the back window of the house. The back door was slightly ajar and you could smell the bread and the food and I imagined I could even smell the warmth, whatever warmth smelled like, everything within the window basking in the warm light of their lamp and their fire.

The door of the cowshed creaked open a crack and a man's voice grunted from the darkness within. She went in and pulled the door behind her. We could hear their voices but the water was loud on the stone and their voices were low and very far away. The voices grew louder, trying to rise above the screeching of the goose, shouting one on top of the other, but still they seemed very far away. There was the sound of wood on metal, and then a loud bang like a bell instantly muffled and the voices were suddenly quiet, closer, and milk came flowing out under the door of the cowshed, tracing out the lines between the cobbles. The milk seemed very white in the darkness and against the blackness of the cobbles. We were finished washing. The milk went on mapping more and more of the yard and the goose went on screeching through it all. We paused, not knowing whether we should knock at the cowshed to thank her. Dan turned and disappeared round the side of the house and we followed and got back into the truck and drove on.

'I'm hungry,' Jack said, as soon as we were driving.

'So am I,' Dan said, 'and what of it?'

We approached the fire. It was a house on fire in the night. Standing in the light of the flames were a dozen life-size figures cast in solid bronze. As we approached we could see beds and bedding and assorted bits of furniture on the edge of the road between the road and the fire. Clothes were scattered on the ditch as if to dry. A stack of wooden boxes had fallen over. There were several men in trench-coats standing back from the crowd, each holding aloft a long pole topped with burning rags, the rags burning with a dirty black smoke and the smoke dissolving into the darkness. One had what looked like a bulldog on a length of rope, stretching the rope tight and leaning forward with its front legs off the ground and barking out an incessant, steady tempo. It sounded like a dog trying to bark, but too hoarse to bark. As we got closer we slowed to a crawl, shamelessly, and I could see other, familiar things lying on the ground roundabout, things you shouldn't expect to see lying on the ground, but which seemed almost as familiar there now as anywhere else. Whatever was built into or fixed onto the walls they had gouged out. Shelves, sinks, boilers, wall-lamps, wracked about the garden. The rest they had broken or dirtied in whatever way they could.

Very close up to the flames, a young woman stood at the doorway of the burning house, solid bronze like the rest. The others were shouting at her but she didn't hear them or wasn't listening. A man came and tried to pull her away and she clattered him in the face and he stood back from her, back near to where he had been. Her face and hands were black from the smoke and the blackened skin was streaked with sweat, furrowing thin veins of bronze down her face, like an overflowing mould in the foundry. Her hands were fastened on a zinc bath still inside the hall, the prow of which was jammed between the door jambs. The bath was piled full with shapes I couldn't identify at that distance and she couldn't get it out. It was simply too big. It must have been a good house because the roof seemed to be of lead or it had lead in it somewhere because the lead was melting and dripping down in globs like rain from the eaves. The rain was on fire and those approaching the woman were more frightened of the lead than of the flames or the heat. We had slowed to watch as we passed and passed at a crawl and didn't look back. I watched Jack out of the corner of my eye to see if he glanced in the wing-mirror but if he did I didn't catch him. Dan was on the far side of Jack, driving, and

I couldn't see him as clearly. It was only a few seconds after-wards that I remembered about the wing-mirror on the passenger side.

'It's very late to be bringing cows back after milking,' Jack said, out of nowhere.

'They were dry stock,' Dan said.

'What are you talking about?' Jack said.

'They were dry stock.'

'I saw them with my own eyes,' Jack said.

'There was nothing underneath.'

'What are you talking about? Are you blind? Jim.'

'I confess it, brothers, my mind was temporarily taken with other matters.'

They permitted themselves a little laugh at this.

'Fucking right it was,' Dan said. 'Jesus Christ.'

I had the feeling that if we stopped the onset of night would stop, that in driving the night lay up ahead and we were driving towards it, deeper into it. We had driven through the evening and now we were driving into the night.

Night

'I'm still hungry after those pints,' I said.

'There's fuck all left, I'm telling you,' Dan said.

'That bread, at the pump,' Jack said.

'I know,' I said. 'Here and see is there anything at all left. Surely she didn't expect us to survive on those few scraps.'

'Savages,' Dan said.

'We're growing lads,' Jack said.

'I'm telling you,' Dan said.

'Where's the bag?'

'Where you put it,' Jack said.

'A lot of fucking good it is there,' Dan said.

I wanted to say something smart about Spenser and Spenser's Tantalus but I couldn't remember the lines and it didn't seem worth the effort and I was sick of trying to be smart about things like Spenser and Spenser's Tantalus. Seneca had a Tantalus too. And who knows how many more.

Dan pulled up in the middle of the road and Jack got out and went round to the driver's side where the trunk was.

'Go on,' I said, nudging Dan's thigh with mine. 'Thou'lt love anon what thou so fear'st to venture on.'

He moved the truck on twenty feet. Jack remained exactly as he was, standing alone in the middle of the road. I had turned around in my seat and Dan too. He couldn't resist. Jack stood and waited and we waited and then he began to walk towards us. He strode towards us with great confidence but without urgency, head down, as though we should be convinced by his confidence. Dan moved the truck on another thirty feet. There was a tap on the roof. He was throwing stones at us. One hit the rear window and we both flinched involuntarily. The stones were loud in the night, even with the engine.

'The bestud,' Dan said and got out of the cab. 'You bestud,' he cried and bent down and picked up a few stones and started flinging them wildly, aiming but flinging so there'd be no chance of hitting the mark.

I slid over into Dan's place and drove off around the bend while they both threw stones at me.

When they came round the corner I was sitting on the lid eating my second sandwich with the bottle of tea we'd made by the river.

'I hope ye like cheese,' I shouted. 'All the ham are gone.'

'Young fella, you better be acting the maggot,' Jack shouted.

The two of them climbed up into the back and sat on either side of me. Jack took a drink of tea and began to investigate the inner mysteries of the sandwiches.

'Here, give us a slug,' Dan said. Jack gave him the bottle and he took a sip and held both his hands around the bottle as if to warm them.

'It's getting chilly now,' he said.

'They've things over will keep tea warm all day,' I said. 'Special bottles.'

'A lot of use they're to us, over there,' Dan said.

'Would you not want to pull her in off the road?' Jack said.

'Sure who'd be so thick as to be driving round the country this time of night?'

'I suppose.'

'Here give us a taste of that.'

Dan passed the tea and I took a mouthful of it. We finished the sandwiches and there was half a one left.

'Who's getting this?' I said.

'Here,' Dan said, 'that savage doesn't need it, he's eating his scabs all day.'

Jack said nothing and stood up with the bottle in his hand: 'Anyone want any more of this?'

We shook our heads. He jerked his hand and a long thin arc of black hung in the blackness and hit the road with a flat splash.

'Alright,' he said, 'pick up your pallets.'

He crumpled up the butcher-paper and wrapped the bottle in it against breaking and put it back into the trunk. Dan slid in behind the wheel again.

We were not long driving again when Jack reached into his jacket and took out a naggin of whiskey. It was dark in the cab and he flicked his fingernail against the glass so that we could hear the glass and knew what it was.

'Our readers would be well advised—' he declared '—to make provisions that on long journeys, locomotive, automotive and such like, some manner of restorative is at all times readily available to them.'

We heard that beautiful sigh of the cork in the dark.

'Did you not get any for yourself?' I inquired.

'I have one answer for you, young man,' said Jack, exhibiting the cork, 'and you know where you can put it.'

He leaned across me and rolled down the window an inch and threw out the cork. There was no going back now.

'Your honour,' I said nobly, 'I withdraw my question.'

'And I withdraw my answer.'

'You beauty,' said Dan.

The whiskey was warm going down and warm inside me and I could feel it moving out through my body towards my extremities, leaving a warm trail as it went. When we had finished the bottle Jack held it over his tongue for a last few drops, then rolled down the window all the way and threw the bottle as high into the air as we could. Hoping, maybe, that it would land where it had been thrown, where the truck had been. We listened for the breaking glass, wondering just how high he'd managed to throw it. Even when it was too late we listened. We were still listening as we came to a crossroads, just beyond which stood a small knot of houses on both sides of the road. Even from before the junction our headlights sketched something in the middle of the road, between the houses, and we slowed and approached it slowly. It was a bull. A black bull standing there four square on its legs, head down and looking up at us from under its brow.

'What a country,' I said.

'Can you get by?' Jack said.

'This is gone beyond a joke now,' Dan said.

The road was narrow between the houses and nothing in the way of a footpath.

'We could back up and turn off,' Dan said. 'Try and go round it.'

'This time of the night,' I said, 'and the man wants to go exploring.'

Dan hit the horn and the horn was brash in the night.

146

'For fucksake Dan there's people in bed this hour of the night,' I said.

'And sleeping,' Jack said.

The bull did not move except to subside an inch or two more so that he was even more firmly rooted. A window to the side suddenly swelled with light and that side of the bull turned to solid brass.

'Here, get out and draw him off to the side so's we can get by,' Dan said.

I was sitting on the outside.

'And meet us back at the ranch,' Jack said, his voice smiling.

'If you think I'm going to put a foot outside this door,' I said.

A front door opened and the whole street warmed in a genial glow. We could see the bull better now. He was very stocky and short in the legs and black every inch of him beneath the brass, with a ring through his nose that looked like part of a doorknocker. The ridge of his back was straight as a table-top from shoulder to tail. He had one little black eye and one eye closed from a wound with a scar on the outside and on the inside a line of wet ran from the tear duct down along the snout to the corner of his mouth like a tear, wet and glistening in the yellow light from the door and the window and the white light of the headlights that was trapped in his good eye. He had two short horns, stumpy and skewed. The eye blinked indifferently and slothfully. A small sheep-dog came from inside the open door and nudged its way past the man standing there looking out and looked out. The dog looked at the bull and sniffed the air and slunk back inside the house again. There were makeshift shutters on many of the windows, some dark, some with brilliant rinds of light between the planks.

The bull sniggered and shook his head brusquely and stood as before. This movement had roused his tail and it swung back and forth loosely like an old swing from a branch. I watched it swing to rest.

'Go on,' Dan said. 'He's harmless.'

'Up owa that, go on!' shouted the man in the doorway, waving a stick.

The bull took no notice. The man stood out onto his doorstep and rattled the stick against the wall. The bull turned his head and considered this distraction most coolly. Another window went yellow in the night and a sash shushed open. Another door opened. I got out moving slowly and smoothly and clicked the door shut and very slothfully walked over to the wall on the bull's blind side. He turned his head a few inches and followed me with his good eye. I walked slow and close to the wall, towards the man with the stick.

'GO ON OWA THAT YE HOOR YE!' the man shouted, much louder than before. The bull jerked his head about and I pressed myself into the wall, wanting to be the wall. He jerked towards me and I ran. I shouldn't have run. I ran in the door. The man was already inside and he slammed the door behind me.

It was as if someone outside was taking a sledgehammer to the door. The hooves sounded and then the whole house shuddered. The second time I heard the hooves I watched the hinges. There was a wide crack in the paint around each of the hinges. The second time the hooves came the crack stretched and shrank again instantly. The third time the hooves came, the crack stretched again and then shrank but didn't shrink as much as before.

'Ye bleddy eejit ye,' he said. 'Why didn't you stay as you were?'

There was no fourth time.

He turned shaking his head and went into a room off the hall. The dog came up shivering in fear and with his tail between his legs and sniffed at my hand hanging down and licked the hand and looked up all sorry and lovesick. He came back into the hall and nodded at the door.

I lifted the latch and opened the door a few inches. The hinges creaked and stuttered.

The man caught hold of the door and jerked it back so hard that I had to step back. He stepped back beyond me, for me to go. Slowly, I moved out onto the doorstep, looking all around. There were a dozen squares of yellow and doors opened all around and the street solid brass and people looking. Someone started to clap and then everyone clapped. Dan and Jack were sitting on the bonnet clapping hard and Jack slapping hard on the bonnet. One of the planks of the door was all splintered. It would look much worse in daylight. I walked down to the truck without looking back. Behind me, I heard the door slam.

'We're getting the fuck out of here now,' I said

In the truck the two of them couldn't stop laughing. It was hard, silent laughter and I knew they were really laughing, not just taking the piss.

'Fuck ye anyway the pair of ye,' I said.

There was no sound, only the sound of the engine and the two of them struggling to breathe. Jack was bent over and slapping his thigh hard. Dan was shaking his head and panting and after a few hundred yards he pulled the truck over. He couldn't drive. He leaned against the door and all but fell out in a heap onto the road. Jack fell over onto the driver's seat onto his side. His eyes were clenched shut and wet and he was whining. Dan was bracing himself against the open door with his head thrown back and his teeth clenched in a diabolical grimace and holding his stomach, looking greatly aggrieved and distressed. I sat there looking at them and nodding my head.

'Go on ye cunts ye,' I said. 'Go on.'

Eventually I got out and went round and pushed Jack over and got in behind the wheel and started the engine. Eventually Dan came round the front, walking stiffly like a sick man and got in and I drove and they still hadn't said anything. Their breaths were heavy and long like runners after a race.

'Anyway,' I said, 'where did it go?'

'Off up the street someplace,' Dan said. 'Fuck it but you didn't run that fast since the minor final. I didn't think you still had it in you.'

'That's it,' I said, 'keep milking it.'

'Classic,' Jack said, shaking his head. 'Classic.'

'What are we going to do for juice?' I said. The needle was getting very low. We'd already used up two spare cans. 'Have you a third can?'

'I have but it's only half full,' Dan said. 'Not even.'

'So? Are you saving it for something?'

'You were white coming out of that door,' Jack said. One Jack was trying to breathe and the other was trying to speak between the breaths. 'You were white as that now, I swear to God.' He reached over and rubbed Dan's shirt between his forefinger and thumb, the shirt grey in the blackness of the cab, no light but what the road and the ditches threw back from the headlights.

I pulled up and got out and reached over and lifted up one of the cans out of the trunk and bounced it up and down and lifted up another one. I lifted this one over the side and went round and filled the tank. I went up and opened the passenger door.

'I'm after losing the cap,' I said.

'To the can?' Dan said.

'To the tank. We've no matches still, I suppose?'

'Fire and oil? What trickery is this?' Jack shouted. 'In time we'll have flames enough to wait on us, brother, without thy aid now.'

'Back her up a bit and leave the lights on,' I said.

Jack slid over and backed up fifteen feet.

I walked up into the white light with my back to the truck and bent over and picked up the cap and went and screwed it in place and put back the can. Jack slid over and I got in and drove.

'That can wasn't even a quarter full I'd say,' I said.

'Did you put every last drop in?' Jack said.

'If ye were saving it for something ye should've told me.'

Dan said nothing.

'Is there any chance of getting any in the next fifteen or twenty miles?' I asked.

'This hour of the night? I don't know, I doubt it,' Dan said.

'No chance at all?'

'I don't know the country. Keep an eye out is all we can do.'

The next five miles we didn't pass a single light and we passed no cars on the road.

'We're fucked if we don't hit something soon,' I said. 'Where's the devil when you need him?'

We drove in silence. I couldn't help looking at the needle.

'How's she doing?' Jack asked.

'About a half-a-mile worse than the last time,' I said. 'And will you stop fucking picking?'

Jack didn't answer.

'Do you want a running commentary?' I said.

'Alright alright,' Jack said.

After another mile Jack said: 'I think the avocado could do with a drop of water.'

'Jesus Christ,' Dan said. 'You're like a sprung barrel.'

I pulled up in the middle of the road and cut the engine as though that would make some difference to the juice but left the lights on. Dan slid out to let Jack out and sat in again. Jack put his back to the lights and dropped his head. He was headless from behind. Dan rolled down the window and stuck out his head.

'Turn around,' he shouted, 'and you might be able to find it.'

The piss started to sizzle on the road and Jack lifted his head and leaned back and waddled about the road preceded by a grandiose arc of piss, glistening and white as milk in the white light. He walked straight up in-between the lights and the bonnet rang metal and hollow.

'The cunt!' Dan shouted and got out and then backed away again as Jack came towards him, pissing. Dan got back in and rolled up the window, quickly. I put on the wipers. Jack was smiling serenely as he pissed, conferring a kind of beatitude on himself.

'Sweet Jesus where's he getting it all from?' Dan asked. 'Where's he keep it?'

The arc died gracefully, like the taps being turned off at a fountain. He came and opened the door and stood buttoning himself up.

'I feel almost human after that now. I tell you, there's nothing more underrated than a good piss or a good shite. Do you know that?' He got in and made a great show of readying himself. 'Let it be known,' he said then, 'the people are ready.'

I turned off the wipers and turned the ignition again and the engine coughed and whinged and died. I tried it a second time. The engine coughed and whinged and kicked in.

'Fuck,' I said.

'Where are we?' Jack said. 'Any notion?'

'Don't look at me,' I said. 'I'm only driving.'

'I don't know,' Dan said. 'Tipperary someplace. I think. I thought we'd of hit Thurles years ago.'

'Thurles only?' Jack said. 'Oh for fucksake.'

'There's nothing we can do about it, only keep going,' I said.

'How much more juice have we?' Jack said.

'You never know with these things. She could have another ten miles in her, she mightn't make it round the corner.'

'But the needle—'

'—that needle has a mind of its own.'

'Thurles,' Jack said, 'I spent a night in Thurles once and I said never again.'

'Was she that bad?' Dan said.

Jack looked at him penitently. 'Well when I saw in the morning what I was after getting up on. Still, we have to do our duty for the species.'

'You're an awful man,' Dan said.

We were in the cab, driving, Dan with his elbow out the window and me with my elbow out and Jack between us leaning back and his arms a crucifixion, resting right along the back of the seat behind our shoulders, and me feeling his arm at the back of my shoulders when I moved or the car jigged on the road and almost forgetting his arm when the road was good for a few minutes and I wasn't jostled in my seat.

'Remember that foxy-haired one he got up on that time up in Dundalk?' Jack said.

'The Temperance dance,' Dan said.

Jack cupped each hand, palm up, and held them out from his chest. Dan nodded:

'He'd ride anything.'

'She was a big girl alright.'

'Slap her thigh and ride in on the wave.'

Without warning we hit a patch of cobbles and the tires chattered loudly and out of nowhere a dispatch-rider passed us, he and his motorcycle blurred and multiplied because of the cobbles. He was travelling at speed and rounded the bend far ahead of us and we didn't see him again.

'He'd've rode anything,' Dan said.

'I asked her what way she remembered him best,' I said

when they were finished laughing. 'Said what she used to look forward to most was him coming home blind drunk. That's what she said. Because then I could go through his pockets for money she said. For food. Money for food.'

Dan dabbed at his breastbone, as he did whenever he passed a church.

'He could be handful alright when he'd a few drinks on him,' he said.

I looked about for the shape of a church or the tall strips of light of the tall windows, but could see none.

'They've done an opera based on it,' Jack said. 'Tragedy with a comic sub-plot. Libretto by Hofmannstal.'

Night

Jack and Dan were no longer looking at the road. There was nothing to look at. I had caught a glimpse of a road-sign and for the first time in a long time I knew exactly where we were. Not knowing, they went on talking as though we still had a lot further to go.

'You know those books of mine he had?' Jack said eventually.

I didn't think Dan knew what he meant, but I didn't say anything.

'You know what he'd done? Remember the way I used sign my name inside the cover? When I was just building up a collection. Inside the cover of every single book—always got your goat, you remember?'

I remembered.

'He'd blotted out all the names. With some class of paint-brush, fine-haired. One even stroke over all the names, every one of them. Didn't even write his own under it then. Just the paint-brush, the one stroke.'

It was soon after that the rain came, without warning. It was a good road and you could see the rain sizzling on the hard surface, not boiling in the mud. Jack and Dan must have thought that meant a village or town nearby and thought we could make it there at least, but it was impossible to see anything that was not directly in the path of the headlights and the town never arrived, as I knew it would not. There was no moon anymore. The headlights threw up a sheet of chicken-wire a few yards ahead of the truck, layers of rain like chicken-wire, layer upon layer, shining in the headlights, blocking our way and blinding us to all up ahead. We drove through the chicken-wire and it cracked and crackled and splintered and drummed on the windshield and on the bonnet and on the roof. You could see nothing beyond the chicken-wire. There was nothing in the world but chicken-wire, but I had slowed when the rain came and slowed now as it grew heavier, as though driving through solid water, slowing for fear there was something out there, beyond the chicken-wire.

'This is madness,' Dan said.

'We won't go much further if it doesn't ease up,' I said, and drove on.

I had seen him glancing at the needle. You could run out of petrol but you couldn't use up the very last of it. All the dirt sank to the bottom of the tank and the very dregs of the dregs would ruin the engine and you'd never clean it out properly again, or to clean it you'd have to start taking it apart, to clean each part separately, and God knows where you'd end up. The good road which should have meant a town nearby had begun several miles back and the town never arrived and there was no sign of any town or village up ahead. By now I was reduced to a crawl. The rain was drumming hard on the roof and on the bonnet and the wipers made no difference. The deltas of rain on the glass gleamed a little of the light from the sheets of chicken-wire and their brilliance, and the rivers washed down the glass even as the wipers made their pass. After a while I slowed almost to a halt and inched over to the very side of the road and crawled along the verge. The screens of chicken-wire lifted and a gateway appeared suddenly to our left and I turned the wheel and the truck settled and was still. I turned the ignition and the lights died and the engine died. What with the drumming on the roof, I had not noticed the engine before, but I noticed it now that it was gone. It was pitch black all around, no moon, no lights in any houses round about, no stars, no constellations of any kind, nothing only the drumming on the roof, twelfth of July drumming, and the three of us sitting in the darkness in the deep-sea silence of a world of drumming. We couldn't see each other but we knew more or less where we were in the darkness.

'There's no point going any further in this,' I said. 'We're going nowhere and if we go any further we'll run smack into something and make shit of ourselves.'

'This is it?' Dan said.

'This is it.'

He took a few seconds to resign himself to his fate.

'Swap with me so, one of you,' he said. It was me he'd been speaking to last.

'Why?'

'I'm going to need to take a piss in the night.'

'How do you know?'

'I always do.'

'Why don't you just go now?'

'In this? I'd be drowned. Anyway, I don't need to go now.'

I could see it wouldn't be worth the effort to argue.

To swap positions, I would need to move over him, letting space for him to shunt under me, using my hands behind me to press myself upwards, and we'd try to get past each other. All kinds of shapes would be waiting for me in the darkness, the wheel, the gear-stick, their perfect geometries, impenetrable and immovable. Of course there was no room and the wheel was everywhere we wanted to be and immediately I was stuck between him and the wheel. Wherever my hands were behind me, that was where he wanted to be, so I had to pull myself forward but I was wary of putting too much weight on my hand and the timing was wrong and Dan too slow and I got stuck again.

'Suffering Christ,' Dan said, 'the weight of him.'

He had to stay where he was and not move until I'd shunted across as far as I could, right over him and let me sit on his lap with my face pushed into the roof and let me get a new grip and lift and lean over further, over Jack, to let him move out from under me and let me fall into the vacated space. We could sort out the legs afterwards. He had to stay where he was till then or we'd never get anywhere. And all by touch, in the dark.

'You alright there, young fella?' Dan said to Jack in the middle of it

'I'm grand,' Jack said. 'Take your time.'

When we were done, Jack struck a match and looked on the floor between his feet. Dan was leaned up against the driver's door and he turned up his collar and snuggled up into his corner and closed his eyes.

'Where'd you get the light?' I said.

Someone on the ferry had given him the box.

The light from the match faded and was gone and there had never been any light. The night was black as ink. What was the line? Where are those stars that were my eyes? Eyes that were my stars? I heard Jack throw the box up on the dash and I could hear him untying his laces and then I heard him settling himself in. I sat there for a long time looking out into the blackness and listening to the rain I could not see. Dan and Jack were soon asleep or if they were not they were quiet and still and their breathing light and shallow.

I woke in the night and the drumming was loud as ever. I could hear the breathing on both sides of me, more laboured now. I woke again later and my back was stiff and my neck was very stiff and my right hand was sore. I sat there a long time thinking I wouldn't be able to get back to sleep but I shifted around, thinking I'd never again sleep, and eventually I must have fallen asleep because I woke again later and the clouds had cleared and now there was a moon and no drumming. The silence was unfamiliar. The moon was a grey varnish on the bonnet and the road and the trees and the fields round about, all dusted with moonlight. Dan had shrugged off his overcoat and it was bunched up between the two of us. The windows of the cab were fogged up from the heat of our bodies. On the condensation inside the windscreen right in front of me, one of them had drawn a huge, primitive phallus with his finger. Which meant that one of them had not drawn it, and would not know if it was me or the other one. Since being drawn the heat of our bodies had layered it over with another layer of condensation, but the image was still more or less distinguishable. I rubbed it out with my palm. Whoever had drawn it would not know which of us had done that. I had to rub it out with my left hand. My right hand was sore and stuck at a strange angle and it was very sore if I moved it in any direction at all. I bent over and with my left hand held Jack in place and as best I could with my right hand I gently eased open the door and held Dan's coat out ahead of me and crawled over Jack, trying not to wake him. My right hand didn't want to do anything at all. I had forgotten about it for a while, drinking, but now it was sore and swollen and stiff. Jack turned and grunted but did not wake. I tried as best I could to hold him in place so that when I closed the door he would rest against it as before. As I was closing the door I had to let go, not to close it on my hand, and he slumped a little against the partially opened door but I pushed it shut and he moved back into place with it and settled himself, a little unsettled, but not woken. I put on the overcoat, which was too big for me, and walked back the road the way we'd come, the road grey in the grey light, the whole world solid granite, and I smelled the wetness of the countryside all about me, washed clean and the air proud with the smell of the wet earth and the wet leaves and the grass and the new blossoms of the trees. The rain was dripping from the trees in the ditch and clinging in drops to the trees, the trees glittering with a million worlds of moonlight preserved in the million raindrops near and far. The distance joined up the drops on the trees in the distance and made of each distant tree a single quivering drop. The water was running in little streams along the side of the road and I could hear it running in other places nearby. I stood in the heavy overcoat and felt with my left hand in the pocket, trying to guess with my fingers what he had in his pocket. Some were easy. I had those things in my own pockets. But others were strange, mystifying, and I couldn't accept that this was Dan's coat. But maybe that was just feeling with the left hand, which felt strange and did not feel like my own hand at all. The mouths of the pockets were narrow and I didn't want to try to fit my right hand in the pocket.

Every now and then a lone cloud would touch the rim of the moon and glow white but there were few clouds in the sky now and the moon was never covered over completely. I wanted to piss but I knew I wouldn't be able to take it out with my right hand. It was strange and awkward unbuttoning and taking it out with my left. My left hand did not feel like my hand either. These tasks were alien to it. It was like trying to write with it. It was like trying to paint with the right. I could have pissed in the middle of the road but I stepped up onto the ditch and started to piss over into the field below. It's much nicer pissing out of doors than in a closet, unless you're pissing up against a wall. Pissing against a wall you get spattered as much as in a bucket. Best of all was pissing into the worm-holes on the beach after the tide had gone out, when we were boys. I leaned back and pissed in a long arc and sighed deeply and freely and something moved right in front of me. About a foot from my crotch a horse's head appeared, considering me and mine with a curious disdain. Probably he was no more happy to have been pissed on by me than by the rain all night. Probably that was why he'd huddled up to the ditch. I jerked back instinctively, wetting myself, and turned aside and squeezed as much out of myself as I could. He was still there when I'd finished, still watching. He watched me wrestle with the buttons again. I fixed myself as best I could and jigged up and down to settle myself. The horse seemed indifferent to the show but he went on watching nevertheless. I went down on my hunkers and held out my left hand to him but he wasn't fooled, he knew it wasn't my hand and turned his head away snobbishly and walked off into the field a few steps. His coat was sopping wet and clung to his sides, his ribs showing through as lines of moonlight on his flank and his mane plastered to his neck and over his forehead and the moonlight shone bluntly on the wet hair. It was balmy in the night and the countryside smelled of the rain and the heat and the night. I looked back at the truck in the moonlight. The truck was covered in catkins from the tree in the ditch beside it, all washed out of the tree by the heavy rain. The catkins were like dead bloated maggots on the ground and on the smooth surface of the truck and in the bed of the truck, on the puddled tarpaulin, some even clinging to the ropes, thousands of long bloated maggots, all solid granite, sodden and rotting where they lay in the grey light.

A lone magpie had hopped along the roofs of the cars, picking at bits of leaves and dirt and debris blown onto the roofs while we waited. The little packets of tea spilt on the road, and the pigeons picking at them. Jack getting out of the moving truck and running alongside to get a bottle of water from the trunk and me putting a little more pressure on the pedal until he came alongside again and then a little more pressure, driving over the packets of tea, catching his eyes in the mirror, and he always coming back, as though this was a race he could win, and then no more pressure but just holding it until he faded away. The drink on the soldier's breath like a strong accent. The soldier wearing a lady's mink hat and ermine-trimmed gloves and armed with what looked to me like a seal rifle. And the magnolias flaking and the man going over the orchard wall and looking back and catching my eye. And the soldier at the roadblock and his scorn. These people, he said, animals, he said, and the stories he had to prove he was right. The one about the man who'd donated his own glass-eye to his greyhound to get a better price for it, and something about women breast-feeding lambs, something I'd heard before, as proof of something else.

All day my left hand had been playing in my own pocket with the chequer I'd stolen from the board left on the bonnet while the players watched the beating, knowing that for years afterwards, every time they had to find a button or bottle-top or penny to replace it, they'd be cursing the one who took it or lost it, whoever he was. But that was someone else. Someone else hearing it, watching it and seeing it. Someone hearing the shower of hailstones rattling on the roof and seeing the little frozen balls of ice netted in the cobwebs in the ditches when we stopped soon after and telling himself to remember not to forget how they looked. Someone noting how the type of walls and the stone of the walls and how they're built all change as you move down the country. Someone alone in the toilet of the bar amazed that there was a shard of mirror on the wall and making faces in the mirror and looking at the different faces and trying to guess the brand of whiskey from the half-letter of gold-leaf on the back of the shard. Someone alone in the cab with the sound of the engine and together in the cab and the silence setting like jelly. Still smelling her perfume when she was gone. Hearing the voice of the man in the shed cold and clear and the air cold and clear, and the lights of houses in the countryside round about and the absence of lights in the countryside. People shapeless beneath coats in cars, waiting. Someone else catching his hand tapping to a jig being scratched out in a nearby house while we were stopped, he who always said he hated jigs and reels and all that. Waiting in the cab and watching them white-washing a cottage across the river, all the dirt, the stains gradually being obliterated, all the time they'd spent putting it on the wall and all the time they'd spend scrubbing it from the clothes. Scrubbing it in the water and taking it out again to look at it. And thinking about the telegram that had told him about his dead brother and how he had kept taking it out of the drawer and looking at it and then putting it back in the drawer forever. All those things I said. All those things I had said. When he was alive and even now. The quotes. I never had anything to say to him so I always quoted myself. Even in letters. They were never particularly good quotes, learned a long time ago, when I was young and someone else, for some future date when I would be called upon to recite them, but I'd only retained their general gist, not the precise words, and it was the precise words, the phrasing, the economy, the actual weight and balance of the words that mattered, the sense that they were being portioned out onto a scale, onto a page. But I was only filling in the gaps and bulking it out and guessing what I couldn't for the life of me remember. I couldn't remember what the right way was but I had no doubt whatsoever in my mind that this was the wrong way and the words felt strange and awkward and rotten in my mouth. 'Rotten in my mouth,' I said aloud, without meaning to. That was a quote too. Something someone had written about his words being like rotten mushrooms in his mouth. His words falling apart in his mouth like rotten mushrooms. Something like that. I can't remember how precisely he put it. And what I'd said about being as safe in an open boat as in your own armchair. *Moby Dick*, such and such a chapter. And all the rest. I could spend my life identifying the quotes.

'Rotten in my mouth,' I had said, aloud, and the sound of my voice brought me back to myself.

I wanted to lie down in the ditch and sleep. The truck was too far away.

After a while I walked back and got back into the truck. Jack had moved over closer to where I had been and I simply pushed him over further. He moved over at the touch of my hand and the night air, as if awake, but said nothing. I got in and settled myself as best I could and waited for sleep and watched what I thought were the first pencil lines of dawn along the ridges of the mountains lying low to the east and told myself I would never sleep again and after a while I slept again.

Morning

It was very bright when I opened my eyes. Jack and I were in the cab twisted and crumpled and Dan was gone and the world was white with light. A knuckle was knocking at the window at my ear. I rubbed my eyes and opened the driver's door and looked out and tried to blink away the brightness. There was a crowd of old men and boys around the truck. The owner of the knuckle was standing back a few feet now, but trying to look in the open door. His face was backed by the sun and the brightness and I could not look at it.

'Morning gentlemen,' he said.

I looked at him, squinting and frowning against the brightness.

'We're going to have to shift ye,' he said.

I sat with one leg inside and one leg out the open door and looked again and got out of the truck very slow and stiff and peered at the crowd round about, rubbing my eyes with my left hand. There were dozens more all along the road to the front and the back of us. It would only be a few minutes later, when I started to get my bearings a bit better, that I'd notice they were all either young boys, still at school, or at least fifty and more. That and the half dozen women amongst them.

'We've a score on here. We're going to have to shift ye,' he said.

'Right this minute?' I said.

'Well we were meant to start at ten.'

'And what clock have you now?'

'Half-past,' he said.

I looked around. Many were looking at me, with a mixture of awe and suspicion, like an anthropological exhibit.

'And you want us off the road completely?'

He wanted us off the road completely. I looked in the gate.

'Can we push it in the field?' I said.

He looked at the truck. 'Is she after giving up on ye?'

'No. There's another one of us,' I looked around, 'someplace around.'

Jack was stirring in the cab. He got out deliberately and delicately, conservative in every movement and squinting and frowning and feeling his head.

'What's the story?' he said.

'There's a score on,' I said.

'Right this minute?' He looked into the audience. 'Where's Dan?'

'Your guess now,' I said.

The gate was a brass bedstead, head and foot, somehow bolted end to end to span the wide gateway.

'Alright,' I said to them, 'but we've been getting a bit of *plamás* from the starter, so maybe we'll just roll her in.'

I got in behind the wheel and the one with the knuckle swung open the bedstead. I turned the wheels where they stood and grunted and turned them again as far as I could and let off the hand-brake. She was well settled in after the rain and only moved an inch or two. All of the old men were standing back on the road, but one of them must have given the word because all at once all the boys moved in behind and to the side of the truck and leaned into it and started to push. There must have been twenty of them or more, all jostling for places to push. The truck started to move forwards, moving quietly and softly over the soft ground. I swung her round wide and straightened her up as we passed between the pillars. We were moving well now and gathering momentum and the boys pushing harder and much faster and further than we'd any real need to go, scrambling in the soft ground and the mud and as I swung it wide and tried to swing it right round they gave one last great heave, letting her roll loosely over the grass. I had swung it round till we were almost facing the gate again and eased on the hand-brake and you could feel the back wheels skidding on the wet grass. I got out and looked at the wheels. There was a two-foot skid behind the back wheels but they were sitting neat on the ground and not sunk in at all. They had pushed us about thirty feet into the field. Around the gate was all chopped up and muddy after cattle, the mud now ploughed with two flat tracks, but they'd pushed us well beyond the mud and onto the grass where we could be sure of the wheels getting a grip when we started again. Facing the gate, I could let off the hand-brake and let it roll down towards the road before firing the engine. Whatever was wrong with the starter, that wouldn't do any harm.

The boys were all beaming and standing around and two were picking themselves up from the ground and studying the long brown streaks along their sides and grimacing and dabbing at the wet cloth. They'd hadn't expected me to swing it round. Some of the boys were looking into the back of the truck. Jack made his way through them and leaned over and opened up the trunk. He rifled through it and closed the lid again. The cupboard was bare. There was a lone donkey braying like a seal at the far corner of the field. The cleanest and quickest way out of the field was along the tyre-tracks left in the mud.

'Dan'll be hopping if he misses it, the score,' I said across to him as we walked out of the field. 'He'll be livid.'

'Have you any smokes left?' he said.

I had smoked the last one during the night. We stood on the road as if waiting for something. The sky was a plate of pristine blue porcelain and the fields of green grain all about shone and shimmered like quicksilver in the sunlight, still damp and shining from the rain, the sunlight white on the wetness. There was a light breeze rippling across the top of the grain and the long grass on the hillsides off in the distance and its rumour moving in the trees on the ditches and in the ditches all along the roadside. Beyond the fields were low hills and beyond them real hills, one with the clean bite of a quarry taken out of it.

'Is there any place around?' Jack said.

'Well, this mob aren't after tramping it from Cork.'

Jack asked one of the men which way to the nearest village. He nodded up ahead, towards where the town was. You couldn't see it from where we were, and for all Jack knew there was just a little village, just round the corner. He asked was there anywhere we could buy something to eat.

'On a Sunday?' the man said, suspicious.

So it was Sunday.

He shouted a name and another man came over.

'These poor craturs are fainting dead away with the hunger,' he smiled. 'What would ye say to a cup of tea lads?'

'I wouldn't say no,' Jack said.

'Here, there's a bottle in the bag.'

I looked him straight in the face and nodded at him in thanks.

It was black without sugar but it was tea and we drank as much and as little as we thought we should. We'd had the tea and were standing there with our hands in our pockets, shifting our weight, waiting and wondering how not to look like you were waiting for something. The first man took out a cigarette and put it between his lips and looked at the two of us. I was trying not to catch his eye but I caught his eye and he held up the case to me. I looked at the case and he held it an inch closer to me and I took one and nodded my thanks again. Nodding the second time changed the first time, as though there was a habit formed or in the forming, ready, the standard thanks, from anyone in my place to anyone in his. I was much happier not having said anything before, just nodding, just once. He held out the case to Jack and Jack took one. Jack started to pat himself down for his matches and I pushed my cigarette between the fingers of my right hand and took his matches out of my breast pocket and tried to strike it on my belt. Jack's hand came out to take over but I put my body in the way and eventually managed to strike it. Shielding it with my right, I held it out to the first man and then Jack and watched how they each took a light from it. I took my own light and watched the flame crawl along the last of the wood towards my fingers, driving a little boiling froth ahead of itself, the water from the wood. The fingers would decide for themselves when to drop it. The first man stood there drawing on his cigarette and looking at us. He nodded towards the truck.

'What's the story?' he said.

'We got caught in the rain in the night and low on juice,' Jack said.

'It was a bad night to be out in it.'

'Is the road not too wet for a score?' Jack asked.

'Ah no, there's great drying there all morning. It'll slow her up a bit alright but she should be grand. She'll do anyway.'

'Are ye after coming far?'

'Dublin,' Jack said.

He was impressed.

There was some movement in those standing in the road up towards the bend, and then the murmur of the crowd swelled and drained away and all along the right hand side of the road, they all took a single step backwards and obediently we did likewise. Normally, this collective step would have been taken with military precision, and something small and black would flicker on the ground in front of us as we whipped our heads round trying to watch it and see it as it skittered low along the road, very tight into the bend, say, and on out of sight. But now we all just stepped back leisurely and watched the bowl trundle past. There was a charitable ripple of applause all round. The springs in the heads cranked them about again to look back towards the start, from where it had come.

'You mean with the coffin?' I said to the first man, nodding towards the truck.

He pushed out his lower lip in a noncommitted way.

'It's the brother, our brother,' I said. 'We're bringing him home to be buried tomorrow morning.'

Now everybody took another lazy step back and we did likewise and the small black thing dithered along even slower again, towards the bend. A slightly more healthy applause trickled back up to and over us from around the corner whence the bowl had gone, to which we in turn added our own applause, though we ourselves couldn't see if this one was any better. We were just applauding the applause, which was a little louder and longer than the first.

He had nothing to say to what I had said and I was glad.

Up at the start, two old men were throwing bowls and two more standing to the side holding the jackets. This was not the competition proper. The pair had paid some nominal sum, a few pence maybe, to throw ten bowls. There was a line chalked across the road where they were and another some two hundred yards away, past us and around the corner, and whichever of the two threw the bowl furthest past the line was the winner. That was the competition. Other men down at the end line, the line around the corner, would roll the two bowls back so that the pair could throw again. Down and back ten times and then we'd have the winner. A bowl came back trundling along the verge almost as quick as it had gone down and Jack put out his foot to stop it. Even though I saw the frailty of this one, I knew what a well-thrown bowl could do to a leg, and felt tug at me the instinct to pull him back. He took it in his hand and threw it back up the road towards the start. His action was a bit stiff, but it wasn't a bad throw. I watched him watching the bowl go on up the road, his face tough with concentration, while he pushed his tongue around his gums, cleaning away the taste of the tea and the night. It wasn't a bad throw at all.

We waited around for a long time more without saying anything much. There seemed to be some problem, of which everyone knew and no one spoke. If so, I wondered what we were waiting for. I thought again of the absence of young men, and thought of various explanations for it. I could imagine trouble in the area, or trouble expected, making many afraid to show their faces. Many, but not all. Equally, I could imagine a fairly comprehensive round-up, but not a complete one. No more than I could imagine that every single one of the men of an age to fight were off doing just that. Still, standing there, knowing the men were looking at us, I wished I were older or younger, like them.

Eventually the man beside us walked up to the corner and joined a circle of men talking there. Jack and I consulted each other dumbly. After a while he came back.

'I don't think we're on for it,' he explained to us.

'How so?' I said.

'There's nobody to play, not for a score proper. There's these jokers of course, but sure I'd throw better myself.' Here he paused. 'Well,' he added then, smiling, 'we do have one. But as the man said, a bird never flew ...'

'The other fella didn't turn up?' I asked.

'Well, neither of them did, to tell you the truth. Nor any of the young lads might usually fill in. No one can throw a half decent bowl anyway. Sure you seen the cut of the rest of us.'

'Where are all the young fellas?' I asked. 'What am I saying, young fellas, sure there's not a man of ye is under the half century or anyway near it, leaving out the *garsúns*. Correct me if I'm wrong.'

'You're not wrong,' he said.

Whatever the story was, he was reluctant to tell us, and didn't want to be pushed to the point where he'd have to refuse us outright. I could see this right away.

Down at the end line there was one more bowl to be returned and an old man was shaping up to break a record. The crowd was gurgling with laughter and urging him on. He was old and heavy and short and his face was bloated and sullied and reddened with years of hard drinking and his hands were swollen with drink.

'I'm going to cut the corner now with this one!' he proclaimed.

He shuffled along a few feet and gave a sort of half-skip and twirled his wrist and the bowl came trundling along by the verge maybe forty or fifty feet. It didn't even run up over the lip of the verge. There were a few lame cheers. Someone else threw it back towards the start and the pair there threw a few more bowls each and then the shout came from down beyond the end line, down around the corner:

'That's the fore now!'

I thought I could see Dan in amongst a crowd of men near the start, and then I saw that it was Dan for sure, making his way towards us. Somehow I thought if he reached us before Jack said anything we might be safe.

'You can throw a handy little bowl,' Jack said to me.

I'd been waiting for that. Just waiting.

'Jesus, that'd be great,' the man said, glad to hear the subject of conversation changed. 'That'd be everything sorted in one.'

'Where were you?' Jack shouted to Dan, approaching.

'Oh, I had a little ... personal business to attend to,' he said, hitching his trousers up in explanation. He was up to us now. 'Well?' he asked the man beside us.

'He's afraid of living up to his reputation,' the man answered.

So he'd known all along, set up to it by Dan. Even so, he'd been too polite to ask me out straight, to put me on the spot. He had let the conversation come round to it of its own accord. Probably they could have got someone else, but now all eyes were on me.

I showed them my right hand, the size of it.

'I'll fuck up my hand,' I said.

'It's already fucked up,' Jack said.

'Listen, I couldn't hold a pen for the tally with it, not to mind the bowl itself.'

Dan was just smiling his way through all of this.

'Go on,' Jack said.

There was something else I'd thought about the night before, in amongst everything else. The last time I'd seen him. The weekend before I was going away, we'd decided to go out to Killiney beach. Walking down the hill towards the sea, we met two friends of his he hadn't seen in years and he decided to have a quick drink with them, saying he'd follow me down in a little while. I went and sat on the beach in my clothes. Three girls appeared from nowhere, bare feet splashing the sand in rehearsal, the wind making paint of their costumes, as the water would later. From the sea's edge two rushed in and soon they were splashing and flailing, as if drowning. But the third proceeded by inches only, arms out for balance, until the waves rode up and down her thighs and she began to ooze whimpers and whines. Then, of course, one of those bigger waves washed up to her waist and set her screeching. She hadn't been expecting it. She turned her back to them, but the waves kept rolling in. First I thought she was screaming out to her friends, for sympathy or incentive, or to herself, or in protest, to whoever was forcing her forwards, or to all of us on the beach, as if in warning or reproof. 'Go on,' shouted a man's voice, behind me. He was one of two men standing behind me, each with a bottle of beer in his hand. The way they held their bottles, themselves—it was all meant to speak of indifference, but their shoes and shirts were already off, and I knew that before long they'd be in the water too. A little while later I went back to look for him.

'Go on,' Jack said again.

I shook my head, and whatever my face said, no one asked again. They began to cajole Jack instead, with Dan leading the assault. Probably they could have got someone else, but now all eyes were on us. Whatever Dan had told them had allowed them to put their hopes in us. Whatever they'd told Dan allowed him to work on Jack ruthlessly now, saying how much the young lads had been looking forward to seeing a good score, what it would mean to them, all that kind of thing, exaggerating so blatantly that there was no point in challenging what he said. Lending itself the effect of something that couldn't be challenged.

'Sure it'll be no contest,' I heard Jack saying, and knew it was already decided, only for the show of protest he had yet to go through. It was a nice little revenge for Dan, however much of the morning he'd spent plotting it.

'Where are you going?' Jack asked, when I was already ten yards off.

'I have a little personal business to attend to,' I shouted, not bothering to turn to face him.

'We'll be starting shortly now, you know that,' his voice came after me.

'Well,' I shouted, 'I may be some time.'

I walked down the road and into the field. In the trunk, there was no more of any newspaper. I bundled and wedged the uniform under my arm so that my body would be between it and the crowd and walked out of the field again.

'Where you going?' Jack shouted again, seeing the direction I was headed in. 'You thinking of walking the last leg?'

'Down this way,' I shouted ahead of myself. 'Where no one can see me.'

After a few minutes, seeing nobody around, I climbed over a gate and walked down the inside of a ditch. About twenty yards down, right up against the ditch, there was a covered well, where I'd be sheltered on two sides at least.

I laid the uniform out on the grass. At twenty, we might have looked something similar, but he'd put on a bit of weight since then, all bad weight and drink. We were the same height, more or less the same in the shoulders, but with him there was a lot further to go round the equator. The adjustable straps at the hips had been fully let out. I wonder when last he'd broken into a sweat. I bloated my belly, stood to attention, filling myself out as much as I could, and held it a while, trying to get the feel of it. When I got tired of the pose, I undid my belt and pulled down my trousers and hunkered down right by the well, so I could grip for the wall support. At first, it wouldn't come, and then it came. With the jacket first and then with the trousers, I wiped myself more thoroughly than I ever did, until I was absolutely clean, taking great care not to wipe anything back onto myself. I was being so careful that I forgot the buckles at the hips and scratched myself, though I didn't seem to break the skin. I had torn off the buttons but forgotten the buckles. Standing again, I could hear the cheers round the corner up ahead, slowly coming closer to me. I stood there listening and found myself picking at the wall of the well and throwing stones down the shaft. I tried not to hear the crowd, listening instead for the stones going down. I pulled off a bigger one, big as my fist. I could hear it bounce off the walls of the shaft, and then the echoes, and the echoes' echoes, but it never hit bottom, not that I could hear. I pulled off a bigger stone again. The same. Nothing beyond the echoes of it going down. When there was nothing bigger to hand, I threw in the uniform and waited, listening, and then walked back to meet the cheers. At first I tried not to smile, and then I gave up trying and walked on smiling and breathing. It was the air of a new morning.

Walking, my right hand had swung back and forth by my side, keeping time, and my left hand should have balanced it. But my left hand couldn't help rehearsing the awkward flick, the way it had of throwing stones. Like an affectation, almost.

I could hear them long before I could see them. It seemed that everything they had to say had to be roared:

'Dan's throw a tuppence!'

'Dan's score a shilling!'

'Shoot the bowl!'

'Bring in the sop!'

After rounding the bend, I climbed up on to the ditch to see over the heads of the crowd. One of the old men who'd attached himself to Dan stood holding a huge handful of grass and looked up at his man a hundred yards off and flung down the sop of grass between his feet and stood with legs spread apart, knees bent, arms raised up in the air in supplication and swinging them down between his legs.

'Shoot her in there now Dan!'

Dan roared something up to his handlers and one of them turned and looked at the sop and at the colossus straddling it. The colossus dragged his foot across the sop and dragged it six inches closer to the side of the road.

'Over the sop now like a rocket!'

'Like a lightning Dan!'

Dan put in a good drive. His supporters were delighted.

'A shilling he won't bate it!'

'A shilling he won't lead!'

After Dan's bowl had gone through, the crowd settled their bets for this shot and turned to face Jack, a clear channel through the bodies funnelling into the boy straddling the sop, as though the crowd itself should funnel the bowl. Seconds later the bowl flew past, along much the same lines as the first. There were cheers from Dan's supporters.

They came strolling down the straight, Jack in his shirt, Dan still in a jumper, each trailed by half-a-dozen others and all falling in as they passed. Jack was talking over his shoulder to the boys all around him and Dan was saying nothing. About

thirty yards past us the road wheeled a little to the right and Dan
bent and picked his bullet out of the grass verge just at the turn.
He held it hidden in his palm by his side and walked back the
way he'd come eight or ten steps with his eyes to the ground.
Dan stood in the middle of the road in the middle of a crowd of
them, silent, oblivious to their words. That is how I remember
him, throughout the match: imperturbable, impassive, wearing
the face of a stoic through it all, apparently indifferent to the
outcome. When he spoke, it would be to convey necessary
information, nothing more. There would be no anxiety, no
disappointment, even when luck went against him. Such
displays would not serve him in any way. He was the one
playing, we would be the ones grimacing and grinning at every
throw, winning and losing for him, who was too busy playing
to win or lose.

Someone had chalked a line across the road where his bowl
had stopped and chalked a P beside the line. I went on around
the corner and stopped just where I would be able to see Dan's
throw. Jack, almost a full bowl behind, had already thrown and
came walking down the road. As he passed he looked up at me
and grinned.

'Are you not putting anything on?'

'Sure I've nothing after the crossing,' I said. 'And even if I
had, I don't know either one of them from Adam.'

How much they'd each put on themselves they didn't tell me
and I didn't ask. They can't have had much left either, not
unless they'd been holding something back at the ferry. Jack
walked on only another forty yards and stood in the grass with
his foot on his bullet.

It was a good road without too many tight turns, a road for
good fast bowling. Dan's drive had given him a good thirty
yards on Jack.

'Ah, he's all the time accurate,' allowed one of Dan's boys.

Saying accurate was not saying fast. His only hope was that consistency might keep him within sight of his man.

'He's looking for a rub off the wall here now.' The wall was all scored and scarred.

'He wants to be up to the pole.'

'I bet he won't win a bowl!'

'I bet he won't lead! A shilling he won't lead!'

'Two bowls of odds!' Dan's supporters were shouting, confident.

'He's giving no ground!'

I was watching the way they threw, the different ways they threw. Dan was serious and all silent intent, playing each camber and bank of the road for all it was worth and edging ahead all the while. Jack looked much more natural and fluid and was nicer to watch. He could be as beautiful and natural as he liked. Now, as I joined them, going into the second quarter he was a full shot behind. His supporters were not happy at all:

'He's just not getting behind his bowl ...'

The jeer: 'Listen boy, the only bowls he'll get behind today is Dan's.'

In anticipation of defeat, the excuses were already coming. The other man was after getting a few nice rubs. Their man was getting bad road-showing. The road didn't suit him. We'd all heard it all before and nobody listened to it.

A few self-appointed officials from amongst the old men did their best to clear a path through the bodies, trying to ensure that neither bowler would have a bowl stopped, but sooner or later it was inevitable. The bowl went skittering across a bend and hit a boy trying to run out of its way, running right into its line. It was bouncing all over the place and he ran right across the line of it and it caught him right on the foot and dropped dead and trundled up onto the verge. If he'd stayed where he was he would've been fine. He was lying on his back on the

road, clawing at his thigh, even though it was his foot. Boys
from the crowd ran over to him and formed another crowd
around him, hiding him, bending over him. They straightened
up again and there was a terrible roar from inside them. 'Leave
him off! Leave him off!' shouted an old man's voice, and they
bent again and shuffled in formation towards the grass and laid
him on the grass. That was Jack's bad luck and it meant thirty
or forty yards less and he was lucky not to have lost more. Still,
there was only a bowl in it and everything still to play for. Of
course Dan's crowd were already telling themselves Jack had
left it too late, telling themselves he'd let Dan go too far adrift,
loud enough for us all to hear.

'He's done enough!'

But Jack seemed to take no notice of having his bowl
stopped. All it was was someone having his bowl stopped. And
the fact that that someone had not been phased seemed to do
something to Dan and Dan's confidence.

Jack's bullet rattled past, clearing the bodies at the last
possible moment, some later than the last moment, only
jumping back after it had already rattled past. The line was
good and some of the young lads began to howl: 'Hi-hi-hi-
hiiii!!' The bowl flirted with the verge but it was confident
flirting and only flirting and stayed out and went on another
good thirty yards and died in the road.

'He was poxed.'

They were whooping and roaring back to him:

'Well on you Jackie boy!'

'Doubt you Jackie boy!'

The bowl wasn't that good, but they wanted to put Dan off,
and were roaring outrageous offers that said the bowl was better
than it was:

'Ten to one he won't bate it!'

'A shilling he won't win a bowl!'

If Dan was to keep his lead going into the last quarter, Jack might lose heart a little, but Jack saw the margin narrowing and seeing the margin narrowing seemed to have given him just the boost he needed. This was the turning point. Like every point was the turning point.

'Play the bowl nice and handy Dan!'

'A tanner he won't bate the gate!'

'He's well high in the gate.'

'He's the gate bate!'

'Well bate!'

Although Dan's bowl only left him with a lead of some thirty odd yards now, it was thirty yards of very useful road, letting Dan's handlers grow extravagant in their confidence, what might have been parody in the mouths of older men:

'A crown he won't get there!'

'Three to the Major's!'

'A shilling on a bowl of odds!'

'A shilling on two bowls of odds!'

Jack's next was a soft bowl round a bend and it needed to be judged well. Jack's supporters were sure that their man had regained the initiative. He played. There was a murmur and immediately everyone began to walk up the road. Someone rooted it out from the ditch and laid it on the verge and marked the road with a chalky stone and a J by the line. The crowd all walked past and on up the road without looking down at the bowl, many walking right over the J so that it was almost obliterated by the time Jack arrived. It had looked like he might draw level before this last throw. He had reduced Dan's lead to less than thirty yards. And now this. Coming up to the three-quarter mark, Jack had not even been a shot in arrears, and now this.

It was Dan to throw and he threw and you hadn't even time

to register what a good throw it was—'A miler!'—before Jack put himself into the lead. Dan was looking as though he'd clinched the score only to have Jack respond instantly with an incredible drive that topped the mark by almost fifteen yards. Everything had changed in a single shot. The crowd stretched down the hill ahead of the bowlers, all eager for a good view of the end.

'That one has done well for him,' they conceded.

Dan knew that any bad shot now would be the shot that lost the score and he put in a very good drive round a double bend, a good combination of speed and accuracy. His supporters went wild.

Jack threw and it was equally good, just rounding the second bend. My neighbour in the ditch and I exchanged looks of appreciation.

'Fuck it,' I said, and went over to one of the men I'd heard shouting for bets against Dan and emptied my pockets into his cupped hands, taking back only the chequer and the buttons. He looked at me and down at the hand with the buttons and back at me, but didn't say anything. He counted it quickly and told me how much was there, as though I might dispute it. The amount didn't much matter to me. Nor which way, on Jack or against him, just to have a stake on, for there to be something at stake. I could feel the muscles in my jaw, tired from smiling and from straining not to smile, like when you're little and sulking against further shame and your father does or says something to make you smile, knowing you don't want to smile, you want to slit his throat because of something he's done, and because now all he'll do is make you smile and because he can make you smile, if only by imitating you and making your shame nothing but a big fat lip. I could feel myself all tight all down my neck and shoulders from smiling. And then the call came, the reprieve:

'Back!' they shouted, the shout relayed over the heads all the way round the bend, the explanation hounding it:

'He's called!'

Dan was claiming that in throwing, Jack had crossed the line reached by his last bowl and the throw would have to be taken again. The one I'd given the money to looked at me again, but I let things stand as they were. Jack threw again and almost matched his first shot. Almost but not quite, not quite rounding all of the second bend.

'He's high but he's not out!'

Even so, Dan would be hard pushed to beat it. I watched him considering the lay-out, watching his face for information about the shot to come, his face blank with concentration, his blank eyes watching the play he was making in his head and about to make. When eventually he played he played his bowl very wide and with a very strong pull, bringing it round the curve and almost up to Jack. His supporters besported themselves like bedlamites. Jack snarled his lips into silent curses, like a bad taste in his mouth. It was like the one with the rotten mushrooms in his mouth and like something else he relates, about a Roman senator crying for the death of his fish, and another senator mocking him, and the senator saying: 'Mock me for crying at the death of my pet fish, you who cried neither at the death of your first nor your second wife.' I hadn't seen Jack that upset since childhood, and even then probably at the like of a dead fish.

Coming into the final quarter, with Dan in the lead, it had still been anyone's score. Now, with Jack just holding the fore, it was still anyone's score, though Dan's next looked by no means a difficult shot round a gentle bend. But Dan lined up and ran and threw awkwardly, putting huge spin on the ball and it spun into the grass not far beyond the bend, far shorter than it should have been.

'Ara he's nothing only all strength.'

'The other man's better accuracy alright.'

'Oh for fucksake, I'd throw better myself.'

Some of the boys shouting for Dan tarried till their man came a little closer to them and then they started to abuse him from a distance.

'For fucksake what you want putting it in there for?'

'Take off that gansey offa you will you!'

He said nothing in return. He was the same as before, saying nothing. When he came within twenty or thirty yards the boys all turned and moved off up the road shaking their heads like old men and conspiring, clotting together and confiding like conspirators. Their man had left himself in an awkward spot, well short of the final bend, leaving himself at incomplete sight and Jack still to throw from thirty very useful yards ahead of him and well into the bend and just at the rise. From that tip a good throw could bring Jack all the way down to the cemetery gates and from the gates a good shot should bring you over the line. Seeing the way he was lining up and having heard their opposites, now—as though equally aged—Jack's boys started to abuse him, as though he'd never in his life thrown a bowl. There was no doubt in their minds as to where the bowl should be laid down. Nor was there any doubt in his mind. He was the one who would win or lose, with this throw. It might not actually win it but it might be the one that lost it. He ran the ball more centre than they'd called for and played slightly right and it went down like a shot. Instant absolution. His supporters identified themselves by their whooping and roaring and general jubilation, while the opposition watched without relish the course the bowl was taking. Loud cries came back from around the corner and moved through the crowd towards us, the cries of those we couldn't see, no more than we could see the bullet. They were the only way of gauging how far the bullet had gone.

Dan was to throw and then they'd each have one last throw. With the end in sight Jack was almost forty yards ahead. Dan was looking at the crowd on the road and seeing the road without the crowd with the same blind eyes and blank face as before, the eyes and face he'd had throughout. He turned and walked back and turned towards us again, gathered himself, ran, and put a devastating bowl into the right-hand track. The bowl flickered along the asphalt and struck the wall away up at the corner and bounced off around the bend, past the gates and right under the line of cars and carts that had been stopped down the road to allow the play. Inch-perfect. He'd dismantled Jack's lead with a single throw, leaving Jack to make up the deficit with his last shot and make it up on hard rising road. So now Jack had the blind eyes, stunned by the long stretch of asphalt that lay between him and the laurels. Jack, being behind, was first to throw, his last throw. Knowing this would be his last throw, Jack gave it everything and hurt his hand. Cradling the right hand in his left, he stood looking after his bowl and listening to the reaction of those around the bend, beyond the line, out of sight. As though you could distinguish the cheers of one side from the other. The cheering went on for a long time. The boys had scrambled up onto the ditches to watch the last shots. Dan considered the road and the crowd covering it and turned his back on them and walked a few yards back the way he'd come, then faced us again. There was total silence. He ran and threw. The crowd split open to let the bowl through and instantly folded in again over its path. It followed much the same line as Jack's. You couldn't see how far it had gone on account of the ditches and the crowd and the bend. From around the bend, the cheering made its way through the crowd, jostling and bullying its way through the bodies, raucous and rowdy and diabolical, steadily making its way back to the start. The cheering swelled about Jack and buoyed him up into the air. Dan's bowl had skidded into the ditch just short of Jack's mark and the boys were bouncing Jack on their shoulders and toying with him now that he had no weight, celebrating the fact that he weighed nothing now that he'd won. But like an echo, another, different cheering washed up around the bend, just as rowdy and diabolical and quickly quenching the first. Dan's bowl had driven through the briars and along the wall of the ditch and stopped a yard beyond Jack's mark. Hats and caps and jackets bloomed above the heads of the crowd.

Half of them were drifting about dolefully, their faces tight and hard and blank and moving like invalids. Jack looked at me over the heads of the boys, like one grief-stricken. Like me, I found out afterwards, he'd put every shilling he'd left, the little he had left, on himself. It was hard not to imitate them, the tight, blank faces. To have carried yourself differently would have been to stand out. Either you rejoiced or mourned and I happened to be in the middle of a group of mourners. After a while the crowd began to disperse. It was all over. Several clots of men, however, remained on the road, studying from various angles the length of road traversed by the last shot.

'Alright,' I said to Jack, 'will we saddle the ponies?'

Noon

There were three ducks sitting on the grass on the sunny side of the truck, two drakes and a duck. They sat on the grass with their feet hidden under them as ducks do and their heads screwed on backwards and their beaks hidden under their wings. The eyes seemed to be closed but then they would move and the light would change on the wet surface and I knew the eyes were not closed. They were tiny, black, wet eyes, welled with water as if on the brink of tears. The males were the beautiful ones and they knew it. Their heads were black and then they moved ever so slightly and the light fell on them another way and they had heads of rich green velvet. The female with her head hidden under her wings looked like a headless obese thrush, although when she moved I could see a little glimpse of violet velvet under the wing. But that was only when she moved and only once.

'Must be water someplace near,' I said.

We'd lost Dan somewhere in the confusion. Eventually he appeared at the gate.

'And he drew near and went with them,' Jack said. That was

the best he could get out of himself. 'We were wondering where you were.'

'Well here I am. Were you watching the score?'

'I was, the second half of it.'

Dan laid a hand on Jack's shoulder. 'Sorry for your troubles,' he said grimly.

'What are we going to do for juice?' I said.

'One of these said he'd give us a lift into the town and give us a drop,' Dan said, nodding towards the road. 'That was the deal.'

'What deal?' I said.

'If we played the score.'

'First I heard of it,' Jack said.

'Well, you can always walk,' Dan said. 'If you don't feel right about it.'

I said I'd wait with the truck. Dan and Jack sat up on the back of a flat-bedded farm-cart with half-a-dozen of the boys, all boisterous again. I watched them move off around the corner, their legs dangling and swinging from the back of the cart. About half an hour later they arrived back with a petrol can.

'Who owns the well?' I said, feeling the weight of it.

'I told them we were going all the way to Fermoy,' Dan said, emptying the can into the tank.

I looked at Dan and held his eye. He must have thought this meant something because he hunched his shoulders in protest:

'I didn't go through all that for a mouthful.'

I said I'd drive and for once nobody had any objections. They knew now how close we were. In the rain they hadn't really been watching the road, relying on me to watch it, and weren't to know till they went into the town and heard or saw what town it was. Dan wanted to try the engine where it stood, for fear of getting caught in the mud at the gate if it didn't start, and having to push from there, but I wanted to get it right first time, to give it the best chance of catching first time and not risk flooding it. They opened the gate and I let off the hand-brake and lined up the wheels with the tracks they'd made coming in and waited till it picked up a little pace before starting the engine. It caught first time and I swung out onto the road and eased up, letting the engine idle. One of the young lads at the score had offered to look under the bonnet, but if we started tinkering with it there in the field God knows where we'd be left, so I thanked him but told him we'd take a proper look at it when we got home, that we weren't too worried once it carried us this last stretch.

A few miles on we were stopped for the last time. These were not soldiers like the others, but had trench-coats and leggings and softened geometries showing through their coats. One of them came over, a young fair-haired man with a thick accent from somewhere like Castletownbere, very different from those at the score. It was the first strong West Cork accent I'd heard in a long time and the words were music in his mouth. He asked us each our name, occupation, age, destination and the purpose of our journey. I was afraid that would only be the start of it but it seemed to be more than enough for him and he nodded us through. I must have been staring at him, waiting for more, even after the nod, because he gave me a wink. I couldn't help but smile and wink back at him. A few hundred yards on, I slowed and stopped and let the engine idle, but kept my hands on the wheel. In all my life, I couldn't remember ever winking at a man before, though I must have done.

'What the fuck are you grinning at?' Jack said.

I couldn't answer him. My jaws were starting to hurt, the way they did when I grinned or stopping myself grinning.

'Like a Barbary ape,' Jack said. 'Look at him.'

'Is there something we should know about?' Dan said.

I couldn't answer him either.

A mile on, to the left of the road was the railway track and beyond it the land sloped down gently and then steeply to a river. Even at noon, there were still traces of mist hanging over the river, glowing with sunlight and slopping over the banks into the fields adjacent. To the right of the road was an old oak woods, sloping gently up the valley, and a rough track leading into them. Between the road and the woods was a narrow strip of land recently planted with some kind of conifer. The conifers were only about two feet high but perfectly formed, miniature versions of what they would become. In a photograph that did not show the bigger trees in the background, I imagine they might have looked fully matured.

I slowed and turned and slowly drove up into the lane. There were stacks of railway sleepers all along the ditches and I nodded at them as we passed.

'Remember those sleepers where they are now. We could do with throwing a few in the back going back to Dublin. For weight. Remember to remind me when we're on the road back, Thursday or whenever it is.'

I drove a few hundred yards into the woods and stopped at a little clearing and we got out. It was not quite so bright and seemed a little more private there. A train passed up at the road. In the middle of the woods we couldn't see or hear it or guess which way it was headed and at first it seemed as though the truck's idling engine was just growing louder, but then we felt it coming up through our feet and inside us and it felt very close and strong and then it was gone.

Jack was combing his hair in the wing-mirror while Dan waited on the mirror and the comb. I stepped out of the shadows to stand in a patch of sunlight while I watched them and waited for them. The trees were tattered with new leaves and three swans passed overhead, going to or coming from a river or lake, I presumed. They flapped their wings with mocking leisure and there was no wind and each flap was a bull-whip whirled in the air.

Waiting, in my left hand I jiggled the buttons up and down, as though they were too hot to handle, as though playing with money. Already the hand was getting into the habit of flicking imaginary stones, discreetly, if it had nothing to occupy it. I could feel the ache in my jaws, as though I was going to start smiling again, though I'd nothing to smile about but the thought of myself smiling. The wrist of my other hand wasn't as bad as it might have been, but the outside of the hand, the knuckles especially, was all bruised and soft scabs, the scabs tearing and bleeding whenever I clenched my fist, to see if they tore or bled.

Between the three of us we knew we could come up with clothes that would do well enough for him. We knew we wouldn't have to worry about any tailor's eyes. No one was going to see him or want to see him after four days, so strictly speaking it didn't matter, but we had seen him and we would remember. Even if we did nothing we had to open the lid again to get back my coat and Jack's coat. We would take back our coats and fold them on our laps in the truck and not mention the smell if there was a smell from them, just roll down the windows and wait for it to fade or for ourselves to get used to it. And since we'd decided to dress him we would remember how we'd dressed him. So we dressed him not in clothes tailored for him specifically, but in those clothes we had between us that fitted him best. Jack had brought another, better shirt for the funeral and took off his own shirt and put that on him, but keeping the collar. If there'd been any sweat from the score it had already dried out. Until we put the shirt on him you could still see vague traces of last year's sun, where his own open collars and rolled-up sleeves had been. We had all three brought our best jackets as well and Dan put his on him. None of us had an extra pair of trousers. I said I thought I was the one closest to him in the waist and the leg. Jack and I were much of a muchness from the waist down but I couldn't help remembering the tar stain from the telegraph pole and I knew I'd remember it afterwards. Besides, Jack had already given his shirt and I'd given nothing. So I said I thought I was closer to him in the leg and that mine had straps at the hips that could be let out, though Jack's had those too. There was a pair of oilskins in the trunk with an inner lining of moleskin which you could unbutton and which I unbuttoned and put on over my underwear. I had felt the moleskin in my hands but it felt different on my legs. The moleskin felt strange and cold at first but it would warm up and do fine till we got to where we were going and I bought another pair or someone lent me one. We could make up a story easy enough and someone would lend me a pair and I'd post them back to him when I got back to Dublin.